one

"That's very impressive jewelry, Todd."

Dr. A. Todd Avery looked at the contents of the padded box with awe. He tentatively touched one of the two rings and nodded. "Incredible. Worth every penny."

"Custom-made to your specifications. I've never seen anything like it."

Todd looked at his boss. Longing painted his features. "If only I could find the right woman to wear them."

"What about the prospect your mother suggested? You're going home for the summer."

Carefully closing the box on the rings and coordinating bracelet, Todd winced. "Mom's really pushing me in that direction. Her attempt to set me up is embarrassing. It makes me feel like a seventeen-year-old in need of a prom date instead of a thirty-five-year-old professional."

"The woman she suggested might be the answer to your prayers."

As he walked out the door, Todd shot back, ". . .or the embodiment of my worst nightmare."

Todd carefully cradled the box in his arm and grabbed his briefcase. He'd stopped by the university's Department of Research for these last two items before heading off to Riverdale. Since he left to attend college, he hadn't been back to his hometown for anything other than brief visits. This summer ought to prove interesting. . .if he could line up the perfect woman.

As he drove, he listened to the cassette tape his secretary

recorded for him. The tape began with her reading the congratulatory notes he had received from several colleagues concerning the successful completion of his last project. Then, she reported a prestigious psychology magazine would be printing his latest article in an upcoming edition.

"I also compiled a list of families with twins in Riverdale for you," her familiar voice continued. "The preliminary survey I did of pediatricians, schools, and churches yielded five possibilities. Astonishingly enough, one name came up on each of the response cards. The mother's name is Amy Wilkins."

A sharp crack of laughter filled the car. "Amy Wilkins?" he said to himself in disbelief. This was the same woman his mother had mentioned. "I don't know who you are, lady, but I surrender! I'm not going to get any peace until I check you out."

Five hours later, Todd reached the outskirts of his old hometown. Things hadn't changed a bit. The elementary school sported a new coat of paint, but the building was still the exact same shades of blue and yellow it had been when he attended twenty-five years ago. A huddled circle of old-timers sat together on the picnic tables at the park, playing chess. The warm feeling of coming home washed over him.

During his sabbatical, he planned to laze around and soak up the comfort while he house-sat for his mom—unless he could locate subjects for his latest project. Never one to be idle, he hoped to begin his research.

Once again, his thoughts returned to Mrs. Amy Wilkins.

Not only would he be rude to drop in unannounced on a prospective subject, such a move would be considered unethical and unprofessional. Still, Todd couldn't repress his curiosity about her. Simply driving by seemed reasonable enough. While waiting for a burger at Fatso's Drive-Thru, he searched through his briefcase for the form where his secretary listed the woman's address. He knew the street, so he resolved to swing by.

Stately trees lined both sides of Willow Lane. Picket fences framed Norman Rockwell-type houses. As he slowly cruised down the street, a pair of dark-haired boys zoomed by on bikes. They were carbon copies of each other. Through his open window, Todd heard them whooping in perfect unison. Elation filled him. He felt like making it a trio. He had only hoped to locate the house—not actually see the kids!

He slowed to a complete crawl and looked at the Wilkinses' place. The woman must employ a gardener. No widow with four boys under the age of eight had the time to mow such a large lawn and plant those flowerbeds.

The tinkling tune of an ice cream truck filled the air. Todd grinned at the realization that the truck still played the same song he remembered from his youth. The front door of the Wilkinses' place opened, and another pair of matching boys rocketed out. Behind them, a woman gracefully followed and called, "Careful! Stay on the curb!"

As she stepped off the porch, the noonday sun revealed a woman who was only in her mid-to-late twenties. Her age surprised him. He expected her to be older. . .thirty, at least. She wore modest, white walking shorts and a blue top. Her cheeks were flushed and her sable curls pleasantly mussed. A soft smile lifted her lips. Her shape was what Todd's mother would term *softig*—not plump, but with soft, overblown curves and a tiny waist. Pretty and feminine, but not fussy-looking at all. Could she be the woman to wear the specialized laser tagging rings and bracelet that he and his boss had admired just a few hours earlier?

By the time she reached the curb, she and the two boys on bikes had rendezvoused. Todd heard her warm laugh as his car coasted past. He wouldn't mind stopping for an ice cream, too; but he had stretched the situation as far as he dared, so he drove on down the street. He glanced in his rearview mirror and saw her buying treats for her sons. Two sets of twins bracketed her.

Statistics darted through his mind. One in every ninety births that weren't the result of fertility drugs turned out to be twins, but only one third of those were identical. That meant one in approximately 270 births yielded identical twins. That woman had not one set, but *two*.

"Mrs. Wilkins," he murmured, "I'll buy ice cream for all of us every single day this summer if you agree to my plan."

❧

"Dan, please stop whistling. My head is killing me. Mike and John, turn off the bath water before the tub overflows." The phone jangled, and Amy winced. Seven thirty. An hour until peace and relative quiet. "Hello," she breathed into the receiver.

"Mrs. Wilkins? Amy Wilkins?"

"Yes, this is she." Amy pinched the receiver between her ear and shoulder as she bent to yank Mike's shirt over his head.

"This is Dr. Avery. I was given your name as a possible candidate to help me in regards to a research project dealing with twin recognition. A preliminary letter, which introduces the study, has probably already reached you."

A vague memory of the letter flitted through her mind. "Just a moment, please—" The name didn't ring a bell, so she braved the trashcan to pluck out the crumpled paper with impressive-looking letterhead. Tomato sauce from supper's sloppy joes gooed up one corner, but she could still make out Dr. Avery's name.

Keeping the receiver between her shoulder and her now-cramping neck, she tugged John's shirt off, too. "Take your socks to the hamper," she whispered. "Yes, well, Dr. Avery, I don't really think—" A waterfall cascaded to the floor over by the sink. Amy groaned inwardly. "Ken, turn the dish drainer around, quick! The water is spilling all over the place! I'm sorry, Dr. Avery. Now where were we?"

"I was going to ask if I could meet you tomorrow, while your boys are in school, so we could review the project. I have your address."

Amy rubbed her aching temple. War whoops sounded from the bathroom. Just as she pivoted around and sought a few polite words to refuse the doctor's proposal, a wet glass slipped out of Ken's hand and shattered all over the floor.

"Good going, doofus!"

"Daniel. . ." Amy's voice held definite reproof.

The doctor said in an understanding tone, "It sounds like I caught you at a bad time."

She sighed. "Listen, Dr. Avery, I have to go. It would be better if you. . . Excuse me. Kenny, Mom will take care of that, buddy. Back away and just use the sponge to wipe off the table."

"Noon tomorrow, Mrs. Wilkins?"

Willing to agree to anything in order to get rid of the intrusive phone call and bring peace to her crumbling world, Amy agreed and hung up the phone. Kenny threw away the research letter, and she didn't even miss it.

Amy managed to sweep up the glass and get the rest of the kitchen squared away as the older boys bathed. After reading to them, saying prayers, and tucking them into bed, she slumped over her sewing machine. She still had work to do.

Her home-based monogramming business was an answer to prayer. Joe's life insurance had provided enough money for Amy to buy a good-sized house with a mammoth backyard. God provided for the rest of their needs through her business and the Social Security checks that came regularly for the boys. The money she earned from these jackets would pay for the boys' soccer lessons this summer. Letting out a small puff of air, Amy turned off the lights, checked the doors, peeked in on the kids, and went to bed. She forgot all about the phone call from Dr. Avery.

The next day, as Amy listened to Christian pop music on the radio and stirred a skillet of ground beef, the doorbell rang. With a sigh, she wiped her hands on a dishtowel and headed for the front door. She stood on tiptoe and peeked through the security spy hole. "Yes? Can I help you?"

A redheaded man turned so she was able to see his face. She couldn't make out his features very well. The scratched glass made everything appear blurry. He cleared his throat, then rumbled in a resonant baritone, "Hello, Mrs. Wilkins. I'm Dr. Avery from the—"

"Oh!" She opened the door at once.

Glancing at his wristwatch, he hesitated. "We did have an appointment, didn't we?"

"I'm sorry! I guess I *did* agree to meet with you. Our meeting completely slipped my mind. I'm so embarrassed!"

"I called at a bad time last night. The confusion is perfectly understandable."

He completely filled the doorway, his bright red hair catching the afternoon sun. Beneath bushy, carrot-red brows, a pair of intelligent, wide-set, gray eyes carried a hopeful gleam. A carefully trimmed mustache dusted his lip, and he gave her a friendly smile. A tie in this heat had to be one of the most ludicrous things she could imagine. Amy stared at him for a tense second, then asked, "May I see your ID?"

"Yes, of course." He set down his briefcase and pulled a wallet out of the pocket of his light gray summer suit pants. He opened it and displayed his driver's license. Amy couldn't help noticing his medical ID lay in the opposite plastic window.

"Thank you, Dr. Avery." Amy still looked at him with

more than a little reticence. Her good manners mandated that she allow him admission. However, she would have much rather slammed and bolted the door. This stranger unsettled her. She covered up her confusion by babbling, "Yes, come in, come in. . . ."

His smile took on a slightly amused flavor as he stepped up and into the entryway. The single step he took to enter the house robbed her of a solid six inches. Amy noted their size difference with dismay. Her heart pounded faster, and she shuffled back a step.

His lips broadened to a full grin as he watched her nervously wipe her hands on a dishtowel. "I did catch you off guard. It looks like you're up to something."

The teakettle began to shrilly whistle. Thankful for the diversion, Amy said, "That kettle will drive us both crazy in about three seconds flat. Please have a seat." She popped into the kitchen, turned off the kettle, and called out loudly, "Can I get you some coffee or tea?"

"Coffee sounds great, thanks," a deep voice said from only a few feet away.

Startled, Amy let out a small shriek and jumped. The teakettle splashed as she set it down with a bang. "Oh, my. You scared me!" She wheeled around. "I didn't expect you to follow me."

Guiding her gently by the wrist, Dr. Avery dipped her hand under the faucet and ran cool water over the small scald. The burn was already turning red. "I'm sorry," he apologized softly. "I didn't mean to surprise you."

"You have. I mean, you did." Amy turned off the water.

He grabbed a dishtowel from the counter and dried off her hand. His touch was gentle and sure. "By the looks of things, you were in the middle of a well-planned, major project here."

Twenty pounds of cooked ground beef sat in a huge bowl.

The meaty scent wafted across the kitchen and mingled with the aroma of the tomato sauce that bubbled on the range. Pints of cottage cheese and bowls of grated mozzarella and cheddar cheese vied for space among the shakers of Parmesan cheese, olives, and three kinds of noodles. Opened cans of enchilada sauce stood beside a small tower of tortillas.

Amy stared down at his big hands. Dread swamped her. Joseph would have knocked her across the room if he had come home to such a mess. This man was huge—a good four inches taller than Joseph had been. Her heart skipped into double-time, and she shivered. Her voice sounded unsteady, "I–I'm sorry."

"No, *I'm* sorry. This burn must smart." He traced around the pea-sized blister forming on the back of her hand. She jerked away and hid her hand from his view. He gave her a baffled look. A tense silence stretched between them until he gestured toward the food. "Do you always do industrial-style cooking?"

Amy warily stepped backward. "About twice a month." She grabbed a box of plastic wrap out of a drawer and began to cover the bowls.

"You aren't packing everything away on my account, are you? I figure you must have your hands pretty full. I can sit here and outline the proposal while you work, if that doesn't bother you."

Relief flooded her. He must not be mad if he made such an offer. She barely had enough time to make everything—if this man would give a quick spiel, then graciously accept her refusal.

"I'd really appreciate that. Let me get your coffee, first. What do you take in it?" She pivoted and opened the cupboard.

"Black is fine, thanks." He pulled out a chair and dragged it over to the far side of the kitchen. "Will I be out of the way over here?"

"Yes. Thank you." Amy was nonplused at his action. From her experience, a thoughtful man was a contradiction in terms. She made Todd a cup of coffee and handed it to him. "So what is it you want?" She strove to keep her voice neutral, but, in truth, she felt horribly jumpy. Nothing would make her happier than for him to stop being so astonishingly polite and just take his leave.

"Do you want the straightforward abbreviated form, or do you want the full academic explanation?" he asked with a quirk of his rusty brow. Amy noted his mustache twitched a bit, too.

She turned away and tried to calm herself. In the background, the words to a song reminded her, "God is my refuge." She whispered a quick prayer, "Dear Lord, please help me today. You know my heart. Help me to do Your will and behave like Your daughter. Give me victory over my fears and keep me safe, I pray. In Jesus' precious name, Amen."

She glanced over her shoulder and realized that he was waiting patiently for an answer to his question. "If you don't mind, I'd rather have you cut to the chase instead of bogging me down with minor details."

"Fine." He took a sip of the coffee and praised, "This tastes as good as it smells. Please, start cooking. Time is one of the three things a mother of twins never seems to have enough of."

Amy sprayed a large pan with a nonstick coating and let her curiosity surface. "What are the other two things?"

"Sleep and patience."

two

Breezy laughter bubbled from Amy's lips. "Have you been spying on me, or have all of my supposed friends and neighbors been blabbing?"

"Experience speaks."

"Oh, do you and Mrs. Avery have twins, too?"

"Please, no," he said, aghast.

"Then you are a twin?"

"I'd best explain: There is no Mrs. Avery, and I am not a twin. I've been doing research for ten years on the subject, and after a decade of in-home observations, those realities seem to be fairly universal."

"I see." In production-line style, Amy started layering noodles, meat, cheese, and sauce into three pieces of glass baking dishes to create pans of lasagna. Todd watched her competent moves. This woman was at home in a kitchen.

"Basically, what I'm trying to get from you is consent to involve you and your sons in a project that I've been curious about for a long time. I'd like to spend their summer vacation observing them for several different things. All of them revolve around individual recognition."

She gasped, "The whole summer?"

Todd sighed to himself. From the moment she asked for identification, he knew that she would not be an easy sell. *She's a cautious woman. Getting her to participate will be difficult.* He pitched his voice low and soothing as he continued, "Since you have two sets of twins, your family is ideal. I would have twice the input for the same amount of observation time."

"But—"

Her dismay came through loud and clear. So did an odd flavor of. . .mistrust? *Very cautious,* he mentally amended his assessment. She needed reassurance, but he'd have to be careful not to push too hard. "Why don't you let me describe the plan?" He waited for her permission. After she nodded hesitantly and continued to make the lasagna, he outlined the project.

"Statistically speaking, identical twins stand a fifty-fifty chance of being called by their correct name. General wisdom dictates that parents fare far better than those odds, but there is not yet any direct, scientific proof. I'd like to place tamperproof wristbands on the boys and have you laser tag them each time you call them by name."

"I fail to see why that would require observation."

Why is she pushing me away so adamantly? She might as well build a big brick fence, she was so definite in her motive to keep a distance between them. Oh, the woman behaved with absolute tact and decorum, but she was obviously doing her best to discourage him.

"True. But that is just the tip of the iceberg."

"Oh." Stripping off a sheet of foil, she covered the first pan of lasagna. The second and third soon followed. As she carried them to the freezer, he stood and opened the appliance door. The cool blast felt heavenly in the midday sizzle and the stuffy heat emanating from the stovetop. He slid a finger under his collar and tugged impatiently.

After stepping away from the freezer, Amy turned on the small kitchen fan and opened another window. Her glossy curls bobbed prettily in the oncoming breeze. Todd made an effort not to stare at her. He lived by a professional code of ethics. Being attracted to a subject defied every precept he held—but something about this woman drew him. Strongly. It was her eyes—those big, blue wells of emotion. There were great depths to her. The music in the background mentioned Christ and God. He had not been around many women who truly lived their beliefs. Many professed Christianity, but their commitment consisted of an occasional trip to church on Easter or Christmas. Her spirituality shone through and intrigued him.

"You're welcome to open the window behind you," she murmured.

"Great!"

"Dr. Avery, I'll ask you to pardon me if this sounds too personal; but I can't help but wonder—aren't you roasting in that jacket and tie?"

"Do you mind?" With her assent, he gratefully shed them.

Grabbing a paring knife, Amy sliced the tops off of several bell peppers. She obviously wanted him to finish his pitch and leave, yet she prodded, "You have a notion that this plan would really show parental accuracy?"

"I'd like to quantitate the percentage of accurate name identification, then see if the skill is transferable. After six weeks of daily observation, I want to see if you can assist me so that I can learn to differentiate the boys to a higher degree of accuracy than the standard statistical probability."

"Good luck," she laughed ruefully. "Their teachers have given up."

"That is one of the more practical applications of the information. Twins who have interchangeable identities seem to have more difficulty in adolescence and major adjustments upon separating as adults. I want to see if we can't help them cultivate individual identities."

Her eyes brightened, and he knew he'd piqued her interest. "You think this research might provide a practical classroom application?"

"Hopefully. I would also like to tally when and why twins

are motivated to fool others. There seem to be three major areas that cause such behaviors: caprice, anger, and the attempt to avoid punishment or unpleasantness. With tamper-proof bands, they can try to fool you, but the bands will still show the truth in the tally."

"That could be interesting." She smiled softly, as if remembering an entertaining memory.

He wanted to ask her to share her thoughts with him, but he needed to sell her on the deal, first. She started to stuff bell peppers and manicotti noodles, so he continued to speak, "There will be provisions for when the boys are generally addressed or when each pair is addressed as well. Many parents of twins hold the concern that they revert to the generic 'you boys' or 'you twins' or 'you guys,' instead of using the individual names."

"I confess, I've wondered about that, myself."

"It would be fun to see, wouldn't it?" he tantalized. "On the phone last night, I picked up that you have a Ken, or Kenny, and a Daniel. Are they of the same set or different?"

"Same," she answered absently as she poured more sauce over the manicotti.

"So you didn't assign rhyming names? To either of the sets?" Hope colored his words.

"No. That would drive me nuts."

"Nonrhyming names simplify things tremendously for the research as well. The boys can't claim they heard their name incorrectly." Todd pointed out salient factors and hoped he was luring this woman into his lair. *She seems easy to work with.* He went on to tell of how several other projects had been waylaid because of the confusion caused by soundalike names. "To have two sets of twins with nonrhyming names in the same family is an answer to a researcher's dreams, you know."

"I see." Obviously, she still wasn't buying his brand of charm.

"I was told they're six and seven-and-a-half. If they look anything alike, determination is probably even more difficult for teachers. What about their clothing? Do you dress them alike?"

Amy laughed. "That was a loaded question if ever I heard one. Why don't you tell me what works best for your research before I answer?"

A guilty grin lifted the corner of Todd's mouth. "Frankly, I like them in different clothing. It allows for a readily identifiable indicator of intent to fool someone. So?" His brows raised in inquiry.

She was far too polite to groan aloud, but he saw how she let out a silent sigh. "Research articles I got from the Parents of Multiples and the library all suggested dressing them separately. Some things are obviously the same—jeans, socks, sweatshirts. I've never made it a practice to dress them or make them dress themselves the same, though."

"Mrs. Wilkins, you have no idea how happy that makes me," he said with zeal. Then, he modified his tone. "Actually, that comment was not just aimed at my research, you know. Your reading was right on target with what our findings confirm time and again. Twins seem individually stronger and healthier when not subjected to the indignity of being dolled up like mannequins. It shows fine parenting on your part."

"I don't know about that." Amy laughed self-consciously. "In a weird way, dressing them differently stretches their wardrobe. The older ones pass anything down that is still wearable, and I fill in the gaps. Both kids just pull out whatever they feel like wearing, so they both eventually wear any one particular article. Since two of any one thing wouldn't stand a chance of surviving, this method turned out to be the best."

"I can believe that. I've noticed boys do awful things to their clothes. The probability of identical shirts or pants surviving through two boys is so vague, I wouldn't bother to calculate it."

"Label it 'never' and you'll be safely accurate," she quipped in a wry tone. "I have to admit, though, that I think Dan seems to be easier on clothes than Ken. The younger two seem about equally destructive."

"With direct observation, I could determine oddities like that. I want to see how much time is spent individually with each boy and how much time is spent generically with all the kids. I also want to see if there is any truth to the parental myth of the good twin/bad twin. If one child is disciplined more often, is it for quantifiable reasons, or is it merely a fable?"

They bantered back and forth as to whether there was really a variance in behavior between the pairs, and Amy asserted she didn't really see that either boy in both sets had more or less need for discipline.

"I think you can see how intriguing it would be to see if the raw data would yield answers to several of these issues," tempted Todd.

"Sounds to me like you're biting off an awfully big mouthful." Two pans of peppers and another three dishes of manicotti went into the freezer. A big bowl of spaghetti went into the refrigerator.

"True," Todd admitted freely. "I figure that as long as I spend time in a home, I ought to compile as much data as possible. Since this research revolves around identification factors, the other information is merely a matter of color-coding interaction on a chart I've devised. It is rather simplistic, but fairly effective, nonetheless." He paused and looked her directly in the eye. "I'd like you to participate."

❧

His project actually intrigued her. He was trying to answer many of the questions she'd pondered and worried about. She decided to try bargaining. He'd opened the gambit proposing daily observation, but she couldn't do that. He might be aiming for far more than he needed so she would counteroffer. She really didn't like having a stranger in the house. The size of this big red giant was certainly imposing. Frightening. She took a deep breath and stepped out in faith. "So I'll gather the information and you'd drop by and check the boys out once a week or so?"

"No." He tilted his head to the side. "I need to see how you interact so I can try to transfer the skill."

Her stomach plummeted. She had proposed as much as she would consider doing.

Dr. Avery's voice sounded unyielding. "I'd need to do wake-to-sleep observations on a daily basis for the entire period of time."

"Every day?" Amy gasped. He hadn't caved in one bit. That cinched it as far as she was concerned. There was no way on earth she would allow this strange man under her roof day in and day out for the whole summer. He had to be insane!

A little afraid to flatly turn him down, she dipped her head and started to make enchiladas. Her hands worked deftly, automatically filling and rolling the tortillas. She hoped her silence conveyed an unwillingness to agree to his plan. Silence stretched between them.

"I know the program must seem overwhelming," he said softly. "Still, I'd leave you and the kids alone each night. If they have any contact with you during my nighttime absence, I'd ask you to keep a nocturnal diary. It would be interesting to note if your level of alertness dictates whether you recognize them."

"Dr. Avery," she spluttered, "I cannot imagine an entire summer—"

She was sure he intentionally misunderstood her when he smoothly inserted, "I am not concerned over the length of time, Mrs. Wilkins. Many of my other studies have been for six months. The time should pass quite quickly. In view of the fact that you have four active boys, I should think this project would be rather entertaining."

"Frankly, Dr. Avery—"

"Todd."

"Frankly, *Todd,* I would appreciate being allowed the courtesy to complete my sentences." She gave him a chilly look.

"My apologies, Mrs. Wilkins. I'm admittedly trying to push myself upon you and your boys. You may not understand what an opportunity this would be for me. It's difficult to isolate causes and relationships. To have only one parent who interacts with two sets of nonrhyming identical twins who are only a year and a half apart in age is an unbelievable set of circumstances. It would eliminate trying to explain why two different families have or do not have the same results. It would double my yield for the time expenditure, and the subjects would be less self-conscious."

"I hold grave concerns about subjecting children to a fishbowl existence, Dr.—Todd." Amy went back to rolling enchiladas. The task allowed her to bow her head and avoid his intense gaze. His eyes were pools of silver, pleading for what she didn't wish to give. It was far too unsettling. *Please, dear Jesus, make him give up and go away. You know I can't bear this. . . .*

"Why not ask the boys how they feel about the study? I've never objected to asking children for their input. Most twins are interested in discovering the answers to some of these mysteries."

Amy's head shot up. In a voice filled with disbelief, she said, "Let me get this straight: You want me to ask my sons if they mind having a stranger stalk them all summer long?"

Todd laughed a full-throated chuckle. His response rattled Amy's nerves. "Stalk them? I hadn't considered it that way at all. The novelty of my presence will wear off after a few days, and the boys will pretty much ignore me. At six and seven, they aren't at ages where privacy is much of an issue. When they turn nine and ten, and certainly during the teen years, limiting access to outsiders is a paramount issue. Right, now they are prime ages for the study—old enough to play pranks, young enough not to mind being observed."

Amy let out a long, choppy sigh. "Your powers of persuasion must have been honed after a decade of practice, Todd." His face lit up, so she hastened to add, "The problem is, you're up against a mother who learned that saying 'no' is the only way she can maintain order and sanity at times."

"I don't intend to upset the order of your home or the emotional well-being of the family unit!"

"I can appreciate the fact that this might not be the intent of your observation. Nevertheless, it might well be the result." The second pan of enchiladas was done. Foil snapped off of the roll and crinkled as Amy folded it over the pans. She carried the pans over to the freezer, and Todd opened the door for her once again. The way he hopped up to help flummoxed her.

"It's hard to believe a woman can carry on an intelligent conversation with a complete stranger, contemplate research, worry over the well-being of her four children, and make eleven meals all at the same time. Yet, this same woman feels that she can't weather someone camping out on the couch, watching her call her kids by name," the doctor teased lightly.

"Eleven?" She cocked a brow, wondering how he'd kept

track when she, herself, hadn't.

"Eleven. Mouthwatering, too."

"I hate to tell you this, Todd, but flattery isn't going to earn my cooperation in this matter. The only thing your smooth-talking will buy is an enchilada lunch. After handling all of this food, I'm starved. Are you up for a couple of enchiladas? I'll nuke them so you don't have to stay long."

"Enchiladas sound terrific."

"Fine." Amy swiftly rolled several more enchiladas into a pan and popped them into the microwave oven. "You obviously haven't been around six- and seven-year-olds if you think you can camp out on a couch," she stated with wisdom borne of experience.

"I was speaking figuratively."

As the microwave hummed, she grabbed a head of lettuce from the refrigerator, washed it with casual grace, and ripped the whole thing to bite-sized pieces in nothing flat. A tomato, the last of the olives, and a cucumber were all thrown into a food processor. She added in a pair of carrots and the machine whirred madly. Amy then tossed the colorful mix into a salad bowl.

"Fastest hands in the state," Todd commented in a tone rich with admiration. "Can I get out plates and dressing?"

"Um. Yeah, thanks." Amy was taken off guard by his willingness to help in the kitchen.

"I saw the plates when you got out the coffee mugs. I assume the salad dressing is in the fridge." He grabbed a pair of plates, threw a handful of salad onto each, covered the bowl with the plastic wrap that sat out on the counter, then popped the remainder of the salad into the refrigerator. He surveyed the bottled dressing in the door. "There's Ranch and Thousand Island. . .what do you like?" When she gave no answer, Todd straightened up and glanced over the door at her. She stared at him, open-mouthed. "Did I do something wrong?"

"Huh? Oh, no. Ranch, please." The microwave buzzer snapped her back into action. "I'm afraid I didn't put the water back on to boil for coffee. Would you rather have lemonade, punch, or ice water?"

"I got a whiff of the lemonade when I opened the door. Smells great. Do you mind?"

Amy laughed. "Not at all. The tree keeps us in lemons all year long. Picking the lemons and juicing them is a good chore for the boys—and I like the vitamin C it provides." She slid three fat enchiladas onto the plate in front of Todd and gave herself two. "If you like them really spicy, you'd better get the hot sauce out of the fridge, too. The boys aren't into the fire-breathing variety of flavor, I'm afraid."

"No, thanks. This will be great. You didn't need to feed me, you know."

Amy drizzled a little dressing onto her salad, then took a bite. After chewing and swallowing, she stated quietly, "Maybe not, but I feel guilty turning you away. After you kindly agreed to let me work while you talked, lunch seemed only fair."

"Don't feel guilty," Todd countered suavely. He sampled the entree and a flicker of appreciation crossed his face. He pointed at the plate with his fork and purred, "As a bachelor, I eat a lot of fast food. This tastes incredible!"

"Dr. Avery—"

Todd burst out laughing.

"Just what do you find so funny?" she asked in an exasperated tone.

He wiped his mouth carefully, then explained, "That was the exact same grave, slightly condemning tone of voice you used with Dan last night when he called Ken a doofus. I can't help wondering if you had the same 'you naughty boy' expression on your face then, too." His eyes sparkled with humor.

"I probably did," she confessed. "You'll have to forgive me. Most of my interactions are with four hairy-legged little hooligans. I guess I was treating you like one of them. I call it my 'peanut butter and jelly mentality.' After six years of being alone with kids, I've strangely shifted into treating the world as if no one else can read or speak in four-syllable words."

After choking down the next bite, Todd let out a healthy guffaw. " 'Peanut butter and jelly mentality?' " His look was one of amused disbelief. "That has to be one of the most novel confessions I've ever heard."

Shrugging, Amy continued to eat. "One of the hazards of single parenthood, I'm afraid."

"If I were here this summer, you might regain part of the adult identity you feel you are missing," he tempted.

"Nice try, but weak," she shot back with a grin.

"You can't blame a guy for trying. Especially after he finds out you can cook like this. Do you have any idea what it is going to do to me, knowing you have eleven meals all made up waiting to be eaten, while my freezer has ice cubes and two frozen pizzas keeping each other company?"

"I understand that the community college offers a bachelors' cooking class."

"You really can handle yourself, can't you?"

"Out of necessity. I have four little guys counting on me, Todd."

"You haven't said how long you've been on your own, but I get a feeling that you're not new on the single parenting scene."

Amy bristled. He'd just stepped into dangerous territory. She clipped out in a tight voice, "My husband was killed the month before Michael and Jonathan were born. We manage."

Whistling under his breath, Todd stayed silent for a moment.

"Sorry. I didn't mean to hit a raw nerve. I guess I'm really plowing in where I don't belong."

"True." Her voice was curt and her mannerisms brusque. "I hate to be rude, but I need to be leaving in about ten minutes to get the boys." She stood up and put their empty plates in the sink. Since she'd cleaned up as she cooked, there was little else to do. She silently prayed that he would understand. She had listened, turned him down, and was now giving him a polite cue to leave and never darken her door again.

"Mrs. Wilkins, don't give me an answer right away. Think the matter over and talk with your sons."

"Dr. Avery, you simply don't understand. I don't see this happening."

"Todd," he corrected her. "I realize that I'm asking you to open your home to a man—a complete stranger, no less—when you have been alone with your sons for the entirety of their conscious memory. My request must seem very unsettling. What I'm asking is that you let the possibilities capture your imagination."

"That, Dr. Avery, is exactly what I am doing—and is precisely why I'm not thrilled with the concept." Amy sighed and pushed back a tendril from her face. The humidity from the cooked noodles made her hair curl even more.

"Will you at least put the proposition before your sons?"

"I suppose it wouldn't hurt," she acquiesced as gracefully as she could under the circumstances.

"Thanks."

His almost-wolfish smile prickled her nerves. "Lest you get the wrong notion, Dr. Avery, I don't run my home like a democracy. Even if the boys all decide that they are of a single mind regarding your proposal, it doesn't mean I'll permit it."

"Mrs. Wilkins, I hope no parent would consider a family unit with such young children to be a democracy when it came to such matters. You seem to have a level head on your shoulders. I never expected you to let the twins make the final determination. I merely thought they might have a perspective that is uniquely their own. After all, they are the ones who live the reality of their constantly mistaken identity."

"Touché."

"I wasn't trying to spar with you, Mrs. Wilkins. I'll take my leave now. I've left a card on your table with the number where you can reach me. I'll be staying in town all summer."

"Very well." Amy glanced over at the small card and imagined chucking it into the trash as soon as he left.

"I appreciated your time," he said gently. "Thank you for the lunch and the conversation. I enjoyed both." Turning quietly on his heel, he gathered up his jacket and tie and left.

Amy crossed over to the table and picked up the card. She glanced at the clock and knew she had just enough time to get to the school to pick up the boys. She turned to toss out the card, but for some odd reason, she tucked it into the side pocket of her purse, instead.

three

"Hey, who owns the black Corvette?" Maise demanded as soon as Amy joined her at the curb by the school.

"Maise Tanks!" Amy hissed.

Giggling, her friend interrupted, "I wasn't spying, Amy. Doc Garvey had a short day, and I came home early. You know I drive down your street to get home. A set of wheels like that is pretty hard to miss! So 'fess up—who belongs to the black beauty?"

"Did you ever think of applying for the FBI or CIA?" Amy tried to fend off the question by teasing.

"They aren't in my league. I graduated from that preschool long ago. I'm still waiting for an answer," she hounded.

Tossing her hands up in mock surrender, Amy stated, "The car belongs to that snoopy research doctor from the university."

"Okay, so you owe me a big one now." Maise gave her a bright smile.

"And just how do you figure that?" Planting her hands on her hips, Amy studied her friend's outrageously pleased expression.

"Simple. Only a single, rich guy drives a car like that. I figure I've done you the favor of a lifetime. He plans on spending all summer at your house and is fascinated with your children. Then, the next step is that he falls head-over-heels in love with their mother and *voilà!* I gave him your name. His mother is a friend of mine. So, just to guarantee he'd connect with you, I told her to be sure he knew how cooperative you'd be. See? I get credit for being the matchmaker."

"You can forget that."

Maise's smile faded. "Oh, come on, Amy. Don't tell me you sent him packing!"

"Of course I sent him packing! They won't want some guy shadowing them all summer."

"Are you sure you're not scared for yourself, Amy?" Maise's lowered voice held gentle censure. "All guys aren't like Joseph."

Amy didn't want to answer. "Here come the kids," she said, evading Maise's comments.

The grilling wasn't over. At the dinner table, John asked, "Mom, the Jacksons' baby-sitter said you had a guy over today who drove a real cool car."

"Not too much salad dressing, Mike. Ken, did you want some more spaghetti?" Why did the neighbors have such a busybody baby-sitter, anyway?

"The *car,* Mom," the boys demanded.

"It was a black Corvette," she answered back. *Couldn't he have driven something a bit more circumspect?*

"Wow!"

"Way cool!"

"So when is the guy going to bring the 'Vette back and give us rides?" Dan asked above the din. His eyes sparkled in anticipation.

"Hold the phone here, guys. Mike, get your elbows off of the table. Dr. Avery isn't coming back."

"Doctor? Are you sick or something?"

"Are you going to die?"

"Who will take care of us?"

Amy was swamped by a myriad of assumptions all at once. Accustomed to listening to human quadraphonic stereo, she heard each statement and filed them away neatly into different compartments. All the while, she hoped Dr. Todd Avery never crossed her path again. "I'm perfectly healthy."

"Then why did the doctor make a house call?" Ken demanded.

"He's not that kind of doctor, Ken. He's a special kind that does certain studies about projects that capture his interest."

"Is he studying you?" John asked. "Did you capture his interest?"

"No!" The word exploded from Amy's mouth. In an effort to calm down, she chided, "John, Dan, chew with your mouths closed. Mike, use your napkin. The fact of the matter is, he talked with me about watching you boys this summer."

"You mean a man baby-sitter with a Corvette? Awesome!" Ken wriggled in his seat with excitement.

"Not a baby-sitter," Amy corrected immediately. "You four, quiet down. I'll give you the scoop." Four spaghetti-smeared faces nodded agreement. "Okay, here goes. Dr. Avery is a man who likes to study all about twins. He wanted to come stay at our house every day for the whole summer and outfit us all with laser-style name tags—"

"Laser!" all four boys shouted with glee.

Amy wanted to groan. She should have anticipated the fascination such a gadget would hold for them. She held up a hand to silence them, then said, "Let me finish."

Kenny tugged on her arm and left a tomato sauce glob on her wrist. "But Mom—*laser!*"

"The laser is not a toy. It's a tool," she told him as she wiped up the mess. "He wants to know if I can tell the differences between you, why and when you fool people, and see if I can teach him to tell you apart."

"That's silly. You can tell us apart," Mike snickered.

"I know, pumpkin." Amy ruffled his hair lovingly.

"Laser tags. Neat!" Ken and Dan said in unison, facing each other.

Amy had a sinking sensation. She'd held misgivings about even discussing the project with the boys.

"We should help him," John declared.

"Will he give me a ride in his fancy car?" asked Mike.

"Whoa!" She rapped on the table to get them to settle down and pay attention. "I didn't tell him yes."

"Why not?" All four boys stared at her as though she'd suddenly grown an extra nose.

"I'm not keen on having someone hanging around all summer," she said lamely.

"Big—" Ken started.

"—Deal," Dan finished the phrase. They did that all of the time, and the habit drove their teacher crazy.

"What is wrong with the idea? Everybody else is here all summer long," Mike pointed out. Amy had to admit he was right. There always seemed to be a surplus of children in her yard. She didn't mind. In fact, she liked it for several reasons. She always knew where the boys were, what they were up to, and with whom they were involved. There weren't many stay-at-home moms in the area, so when her boys went elsewhere, the baby-sitters weren't always of the quality that made her feel comfortable. After having had a lousy childhood herself, she enjoyed providing her boys with a happy one. Other kids gravitated to their house as a natural result. "There is a big difference between having friends over and having an adult observe you," Amy stated simply.

"What's the difference? He could even out the teams when we shoot hoops," Ken pointed out.

"And when we do baseball and races," John agreed, again finishing his brother's sentence.

"Wait a second, guys. Dr. Avery wouldn't come as a playmate. He would come to observe and study you. At least, that's my understanding." Suddenly, the thought occurred to her that Dr. Avery hadn't outlined the extent of his involvement. She shook her head. Oh, well. It was a moot point, anyway.

"Too bad," Mike lamented. "Still, I think it's okay for him to sit around. It wouldn't hurt anything, would it?"

"Of course it wouldn't hurt anything, goofball!" Ken chided.

"So why does he sit around and study kids anyway?" Dan chonked into another piece of garlic bread.

"Not such big bites, Danny."

"He can handle it, Mom. He has a big mouth!" Kenny teased good-naturedly.

"No bigger than yours," Dan shot back.

"Boys!" Amy glared at them, and they had the good sense to settled back down. "The rule in this house is love. Let kindness lead your tongue."

"Why does he study kids, Mom?" John repeated his older brother's query.

"Dr. Avery studies twins. He thinks maybe there's a way to teach other people how to tell you apart the way I do."

"No foolin'?"

"No fooling," Amy laughed at his wide-eyed expression.

"How come you can and nobody else does?" Ken asked.

"Somebody else does tell you apart," she replied. "You boys don't mix each other up. Ken and Dan don't mix up John and Mike, and vice versa."

"What does vice versa mean?" Mike wanted to know.

"It means the turnaround, you know—the opposite. In this case, it means that you and John don't mix up Ken and Dan."

"Of course we don't," John asserted in a huff.

"I always thought it was weird that we could tell each other apart and nobody else could," admitted Ken.

"Yeah. It would be kinda important if we could help him figure out how to do it, wouldn't it?" Dan asked.

"Let's do it!" Mike and John chorused.

Shaking her head at the mess she had gotten into, Amy put down her fork. "I pretty much made up my mind against it, team. I'll give it a bit of thought for a few days, but don't get your hopes up. I've already told you—I'm not keen on having someone hang around in the shade all summer."

"But Mom. . ."

Holding up a hand to signal that the topic was closed, Amy stated, "I've heard enough on this subject. Now do your chores and get ready for bed. I, for one, want to read what David does in the next chapter. Last night's story left us hanging." She reminded the boys of the cliff-hanging ending of the Bible story regarding David and Jonathan, and they sprang into action. John cleared the table while Mike swept the floor. The older boys washed and dried the dishes while the younger two bathed. While they worked, Amy quizzed them on the next day's spelling test. When they went to shower, she quizzed the younger set. Life had to go on, and she wanted to keep busy. She didn't want to think about the unsettling doctor.

❧

Just after lunch the next afternoon, the phone rang. The school secretary was on the line. "Mrs. Wilkins, could you please come down to the school? We seem to have a small problem."

"Is one of the boys hurt?" She frantically reached for her keys.

"Oh, no." Amy sighed in relief, then frowned at the follow-up. "One is in trouble, but we aren't sure which one to discipline!"

"I'll be right there." Grabbing her purse, she flew out of the door and off to the school.

Ken and Dan were both sitting on a bench outside of the principal's office. As soon as Amy arrived, all three of them were ushered into the office. Amy sat thin-lipped and stiff.

"I'm sorry to have to bother you, Mrs. Wilkins, but this is a rather unique problem. We take pride in disciplining fairly, but we ran into a snag here." Mr. Frobisher looked a bit embarrassed over the incident. "It seems Miss Nadeaux was showing a film and one of the boys indulged in shooting spitballs across the classroom. Since the room was dim and both boys are wearing dark shirts, she wasn't sure which one was responsible for the offense."

Amy turned and looked at both boys. "Daniel James Wilkins, you have some explaining to do. "Ken, I'll talk with you in a minute."

"I'm sorry, Mom," Dan grumbled under his breath. "The movie was really boring. We already saw it last year."

"That was no reason for such behavior." Amy was unyielding. She turned to Mr. Frobisher. "What is the usual punishment for this?"

"Twenty minutes of detention."

"Daniel, you will stay in detention for thirty minutes because you caused your brother embarrassment *and*," Amy added, "during that time you are to make me one hundred spitballs. Prime quality spitballs. Do you understand me?"

"Yes, Mom."

Amy glared at her second son. "Kenneth Andrew, did you give the teacher any reason to believe that you were somehow involved in this escapade?"

"I didn't tell her I didn't do it," he admitted slowly. "But, Mom, she didn't ask. She just got mad and made us both come to the office right away!"

"Did you do anything to make her think that you might have done it?"

"No." His face had a stricken look.

"Mom, this isn't fair," Dan objected. "It wasn't his fault at all. Miss Nadeaux got mad 'cuz she couldn't tell us apart. She didn't even try to find out whose fault it was. He shouldn't get in trouble because of me."

"Why didn't you tell Principal Frobisher this was your fault and save your brother the hassle?"

"I was scared of him!" came the wail. "Nobody else has to come here if they make spitballs!"

"I see." Amy looked to the principal for confirmation. He nodded wryly. "You boys go on back to class. Daniel, stop and ask the secretary for an envelope for those spitballs you'll be making." She leaned forward and hugged each boy as they left.

Kenny begged quietly, "Mommy, let the man come so I don't get into trouble like this again. I want the teacher to tell us apart!"

"I'll think about it," she promised. After the boys were gone, Amy sat in silence as she took a moment to pray for wisdom. She drew a deep breath to control her anger and asked, "Mr. Frobisher, does Miss Nadeaux have a problem with her students making spitballs?"

"Actually, there seems to, um. . .have been a rash of them in that grade," he admitted.

"And have any of the other offenders been sent to the office to be punished by you?"

"No."

"So my sons were singled out for that particular ignominy, and the teacher knew full well that one was entirely innocent?" Her voice was deceptively calm. As a mother, she wanted to rant and rave; but as a Christian, she knew she needed to mind her witness.

"I suppose you could say that."

"I see." Silence stretched for a moment again. In an eerily calm tone she continued, "Let me see if I can encapsulate this whole affair. One of my two sons created a common disturbance. Because they are difficult to distinguish, the teacher made no effort whatsoever to ascertain who the guilty party was. Instead, she singled them out for a punishment usually reserved for major problems. Does that sum up the situation fairly?"

Clearing his throat, the principal agreed, "I think that is an accurate summary."

"Mr. Frobisher, my sons pose a unique challenge to your staff in that they are twins; however, since you have but one class for each grade, it's impossible to separate them. They dress differently, and I should think that, alone, would make it easier for their teacher to distinguish them. I have to grudgingly honor Ken for standing beside his brother and giving him moral support in the face of the overwhelming punishment that was meted out. It would have been easy for him to protest his innocence and tattle. He didn't do so. When faced with his crime, Dan admitted it freely and exonerated his brother. Why were you and his teacher unable to elicit this information?"

"Frankly, Mrs. Wilkins, I haven't the vaguest notion of how you knew which was which, let alone who was the guilty party." The admission was made shamefacedly.

"Daniel's face and posture gave him away. There was no doubt about it."

"That makes sense. I must apologize to you for the fact that their teacher made no effort to determine who was at fault. That wasn't transmitted to me."

"I'll thank you to discuss the matter with her," Amy stated firmly.

"And so I shall. Still, I must ask: How did you know the one wearing the guilty look was Daniel?"

Amy shrugged. "How do you know your left arm from your right?"

"You continually amaze me," the man sighed. "Mrs. Wilkins, I wonder about something else as well." Her raised brows invited him to continue on. "Why the hundred spitballs?"

She let out a peal of laughter. "Mr. Frobisher, after making a hundred spitballs in thirty minutes, I doubt Daniel will have any desire to make another one for a long, long time. It seems like an insurance policy to me. His teacher won't have to deal with this behavior from him for the next week until school lets out."

There was almost an hour left before the end of school. Amy went for a walk. Kenny's plea rang in her ears. "Please, Mommy, let the man come. . . ." He had to have been terribly upset to call her "Mommy." The boys had given that up upon entering kindergarten. It was always "Mom" or on occasion "Mother" if a homemade card was involved.

What would it be like to have other people give her sons the gift of individuality? It would be a victory of sorts. Twins shared something unique and special—built-in playmates and confidants and probably more than their share of public attention. Yet, on the downside, once familiar with them, others tended to group them as an inseparable pair, robbing them of the joy of single friendships or their rightful names and identities.

Often the boys were given a single card and gift on their birthdays. Amy always found it hard to explain to them that a single truck or hockey stick was supposed to be a shared gift. Frisbees, balls, and building sets were understandable. She felt that it was thoughtless, cruel, or even downright cheap of people to lump the twins together as though they had but one set of arms and legs. Other mothers in the Parents of Multiples club complained of the same kind of problems.

Today's mix-up was like the icing on the cake. A teacher who punished both for the infraction of one and didn't even try to sort the two out. . .and her punishment was extreme. Amy wanted to believe that today's incident was an isolated one, but she couldn't fool herself. This was a teacher who had been quite impressive. She simply reacted in sheer frustration.

Amy's heart ached for both of her sons. Kenny was unjustly accused and punished, and Daniel had twice the guilt and extreme punishment for a minor infraction.

Could Dr. Avery's research make a difference? Even if his findings only worked for her sons and no other sets of identicals, would it be worth the loss of her privacy if others could be taught to distinguish her children? The doctor's pointers might give them the gift of their own identities. The most painful question she had to ask herself was whether Maise was right. By turning down the study, was she putting her own fears above her sons' welfare? It was an appalling thought.

A whole summer with that man underfoot. *No, overhead,* she corrected herself with a twisted grimace. He was huge! The loss of privacy obviously wouldn't bother the boys. They were extroverted children and didn't possess a scrap of modesty among the lot of them. In another year or two, that would definitely change. He had been right about that. It was now or never. But could *she* handle having him around? Honestly, she held grave doubts; but as a parent, she needed to put her children's needs above her own comfort.

She sat on a park bench and clasped her hands tightly in her lap. *Lord, I don't know what to do. Is this Your will? Do I take this chance? You promise to give wisdom, and I'm pleading with You to grant me insight. Help me be a good mother. Please, Father, give me a sense of direction.*

A dapper old man came and sat at the other end of the bench. He opened the small bag he'd brought and started to cast breadcrumbs onto the pavement. "The sparrows and chickadees won't need me to come here once the school year ends," he confided. "Everyone comes here, and my little friends all snack on the food the children leave behind."

Amy sat and watched the mud-colored birds hop and peck. "They all look alike to me," she confessed. "How do you tell them apart?"

"Oh, they're different. The chickadee is fatter. See that one, there? He's a sparrow. At first, you might have to compare size, but after awhile, you can just look and tell."

Amy sat and stared down at the birds in stunned silence. She'd prayed for an answer. God's bidding seemed so very clear. It was as if she had just lived a parable. There really was no decision to be made, after all. She fished in her purse for some change and walked to a pay phone. It was better to get this over with before she lost her faith and resolve.

⫷

Todd hung up the phone and let out a joyous whoop. He hadn't held much hope of Amy Wilkins assenting to the study. After he had left her kitchen, he'd known she was too wary to have him come and do the study. She valued her privacy far too much. The last thing he ever expected was to have her call him and give her consent to the plan.

She had been less than positive on the phone, but she gave her approval. With time, she would come to accept his presence if he would just stay calm and cool around her. A huge grin danced across his face—she wasn't here, so he could let loose. He was more excited about this project than he had been about any other that he could think of. He dialed one of his colleagues at the university. He had to boast about this coup.

Todd suggested that he meet the boys and give them a chance to get to know him firsthand before he became a permanent fixture around the house. He wanted to show them the tagging system and answer questions so everyone would start with the same basic information.

"I'm sorry, but next week is the last week of school," Amy had said. "We have something almost every night, and I've already promised to take them swimming on Saturday. And the church picnic is Sunday after services."

"You aren't exactly the dull, boring, stay-at-home domestic breed, are you?" he teased.

"You did say that you didn't want us altering our lifestyle."

"And I still don't. Do you have any objection to me tagging along at the church picnic? I'm house-sitting this summer for my mom. She's going to Europe. I'm supposed to see her off at the airport on Saturday."

Amy was completely taken by surprise. "I guess you could come. The whole community is invited." It was far from an open-ended, gracious invitation; but it was the best she could manage, given her less than hospitable feelings.

"Sounds like fun. What do you want me to bring?"

"Nothing."

"You're no fun, Mrs. Wilkins. A baseball mitt? Watermelon? Blankets and a Frisbee?"

"They'll probably play baseball after lunch. There will be food enough for a small army, so don't even think about bringing a thing to eat."

"Okay. I'll bring my old baseball glove and see you then. When I was a boy, we used to wear our jeans to church on picnic Sundays instead of changing between services and the picnic. Is that still acceptable?"

"Jeans are fine. I'd like to know something, though. Just how long has it been since you went to church, Todd?"

"Can't say that I have an exact answer. A long time. Why?"

"Ours is a Christian home. We live by the Bible, and I insist upon decent language and conduct. We haven't discussed that matter, and I feel I must say something now. It's too important to me to have the boys reared in a godly manner. If you have a problem with this, I'll ask you to be honest with me so we can part ways now." He heard her take in a deep breath and gush in a guilty tone, "I should have asked all of this before I agreed."

He could hear the wheels turning in her mind. This was her last-ditch effort to escape. He wasn't about to let her. "I don't know that you could exactly paint me as a heathen, but I'll admit that I haven't attended church for a while. It would be nice to get back into the swing of things."

There was a long silence. In a muted voice, she asked, "Then, Jesus Christ isn't your personal Savior?"

"I made a commitment back when I was in junior high. Somewhere in college, I stopped going to church and reading my Bible. I'll certainly attend with you and honor your beliefs."

"I'm sorry, Todd. I hope I didn't sound too judgmental. You have the right to live according to the dictates of your heart."

"And you have a responsibility to be sure that your sons aren't subjected to bad role models," he soothed. "I took no offense."

He could just picture her, her eyes closed and her shoulders drooping as she let out a long, slow sigh. Professional experience made him certain the boys wouldn't mind his presence, but she was a woman who prized her privacy. She was making a huge sacrifice in hopes that this might somehow benefit her sons.

In a muted tone, she said, "The church picnic might be a good way for the kids to meet you."

"Fine. Mrs. Wilkins, I want to thank you in advance for allowing me into your home. I'll do my best to be unobtrusive." He hastened to end the conversation before she could lose her nerve and change her mind. "I'll meet you at church on Sunday. I just need to ask one last question: What is your ring size?"

"My ring size?"

"Yes. The laser equipment will have rings. I'd like to have them customized for your comfort."

"Oh. I'm not sure."

He thought of asking about her wedding ring, but something held him back. He'd noticed she didn't wear one. Many widows didn't. Perhaps her memories were too painful, and he didn't want to upset her. "It's okay. We'll have time to measure you later. Thank you for calling. I'll see you Sunday."

❧

After sending his mom off to Europe, Todd left town and drove back to his apartment to pack up what he would need for the summer. He had already brought down his computer, the necessary software, and his briefcase. A few resource books, some sports equipment, shorts, shirts, and jeans would suffice.

He hired a housekeeping company to send someone over to his apartment once a week to dust and tidy up the place. He felt comfortable leaving a key with them. After all, they were licensed and bonded. They had proven to be conscientious when he'd been absent during other in-home observations. The fact of the matter was, his apartment was just a way station. He didn't spend much time there, and the place lacked any warmth or hominess. As he glanced about one last time, the thought struck him—his place was just as cold as Amy Wilkins's home was warm.

❧

"Church sure has changed!" Todd declared as he sat down on the blanket across from Amy. He'd been pleasantly surprised by the number of young families now attending the church and enjoyed the updated music featured in the service. Precariously balancing his heavily laden plate, Todd lowered himself onto the blanket. He settled his long legs over the edge and kept his feet on the grass. "Yep. Church has changed," he repeated.

"But the picnic hasn't, right?"

He looked down at his plate and laughed. "Neither has my appetite. Lacy Smith still makes deadly potato salad."

"Yeah, but I'm looking forward to eating the pie," Dan stated, eyeing the dessert table with desire.

"I'm going for that chocolate cream," Ken decided, his mouth full of fried chicken.

"Mom, can we have apple and cherry pie both?" one son pled for himself and his brother.

"John, you may have only one. If Mike happens to choose the opposite and you trade plates halfway through the piece, you'll be happy enough."

"Awww, Mom, are you sure?"

"Yes, young man. No pie at all if you don't finish the main course first. Ken, please chew with your mouth closed."

Todd ate with relish as he took in his surroundings, paying particularly close attention to Amy's interaction with her sons. In the last ten minutes, she had helped them pile food on their plates, located their favorite dishes, and cajoled them into making a fairly well balanced selection. She addressed them in all sorts of different ways. He would need to catalogue them all—she used their individual names frequently, but nicknames and generic calls also abounded.

The boys had exercised passable manners upon being introduced, then were polite enough to thank Todd for having gotten them all cups of punch. Amy had gawked at him for carrying over the drinks. Thinking of one of the families he had observed that didn't allow drinks until after the meal was over, he asked, "Do the boys usually wait for their drinks until after they've eaten so you make sure they eat well?"

"No," she had answered hesitantly. She shook her head and

gave him a strained smile. "Thanks for getting the punch."

"No sweat. I'll stay put for a second while you go get some grub," he offered.

"The boys will be okay here."

"Afraid to leave them alone with me?" he asked quietly so no one else could hear him. Her strangled gasp was answer enough. "Okay, Amy, we'll go together." He had taken longer to fill his plate, but noticed how she carefully chose more· of the fruits and salads. Now he noted that she wasn't entering in on the bids for which dessert she was going to nab. "What are you going to have for dessert, Amy?" he asked nonchalantly.

"I can tell you what she'll pick without even looking at the dessert table," Dan bragged. "She'll eat Mrs. Cama's awful pudding."

"It's icky," confided Mike.

"Oh?"

"I like it." Color mounted in Amy's cheeks.

"Maybe I ought to try some to make up my own mind," Todd stated.

Kenny warned with a grimace, "Get ready to gag."

"Any more of that kind of talk, and all four of you will go without dessert at all," Amy warned in a steely tone. She leaned forward just slightly. "Mrs. Cama is diabetic. Her dessert is sugar-free."

"I see," Todd mused. Sugar-free dessert and a low-fat, low-calorie lunch. Did Amy happen to be dieting? Was this a social issue as it was with several women when they ate publicly? Or did she just have a food preference that went toward such choices?

Ken broke into his musings. "Are you going to play baseball?"

"Maybe I'll play in the second half. I'll stick around to help tie you guys up for the three-legged races, okay?"

"Are you going to do the wheelbarrow race or the gunny sack race?"

Todd looked over and tried to decide whether it was Mike or John that had asked. "Which one of you asked me that?"

"I did," they both answered. They exchanged looks and laughed merrily.

"Caprice." He shot a grin at Amy and snaked over both hands, tickling both small boys simultaneously. "You'll both pay the price for your joke, then."

"Why did you phrase it that way?" Amy inquired. "Most people would have asked *who* had asked."

"Two reasons. I wanted to give them an opening for capricious play to see if they'd bite. They did. The other reason was that since their voices sound identical to me at this point, I want to see if I can judge inflection and identity on my own."

"Okay. I get you. This is the one who spoke." She tapped the chest of one of the giggling boys.

"Mike?"

"What makes you think this is Mike?" Amy asked, tilting her head to one side and shaking it negatively.

"My only clue is that Mike was wearing that shirt when you introduced us."

"Wrong!" The boys rolled on the grass in amusement. "We swapped while you were getting your food!"

"Caprice," Amy reiterated.

"Did you see them doing it?" Todd grilled her intently.

"Nope."

"Did you know?"

"Of course I knew." She looked up at him and shrugged. "I can anticipate your next question. No, I haven't the slightest idea as to how I knew they had traded shirts. I just did."

"When did you realize it?"

"When?" She looked puzzled.

"Yeah. Did you know five feet away, or when you first sat down, or three minutes later?"

"I don't recall. When I sat down, I guess. Why? What difference does it make?"

"I wondered what clued you in—their collective behavior? Facial expressions? Voice differences? Or some vague physical difference."

Amy stared at him and wrinkled her nose. "I'm not exactly sure," she admitted slowly.

"Can we go get our pie now?"

"Sure, Dan. Take Mike with you. Ken, will you please help Johnny?"

"You didn't even look. How did you know it was Dan?" Todd quizzed.

"I think you are going to give me a world class headache, Dr. Avery."

By the end of the day, the boys were totally taken with the good doctor. Todd insisted on them calling him by his first name, and Amy grudgingly permitted the informality. It made perfect sense, but she was reticent to call him by his given name as well. It made him seem like a friend, and she wasn't sure she was ready for that.

After helping with the kids' races, Todd played baseball. He was skilled at both locations. The boys were already asking him for batting tips after watching him crack one way out of the field. Todd Avery hadn't even started his study, yet he was taking over her children and her sanity like Rommel trounced through Africa.

four

The doorbell rang and Amy opened one eye to look at the clock before she rolled over and pulled the pillow over her head. Six A.M. on Saturday morning. The clock read six A.M. Who would be so insane as to come to her door at such an early hour? She let out a muffled groan, yawned, and burrowed her cheek into the flower-sprigged percale bed sheet.

"Mom, some guy is on the porch," Mike announced from her door.

"Tell him to go away," she mumbled.

"Wow!" Johnny's voice bellowed at top volume from downstairs.

Seconds later, a much deeper voice sounded from her doorway, "I bribed my way inside with doughnuts. I'm here to band the kids—"

Amy shrieked and bolted upright, clutching the blankets up to her neck. She and the intrusive visitor stared at each other. "Dr. Avery! What are you doing here?"

"It's Saturday—"

"Exactly!"

"School ended yesterday, didn't it?" Todd asked.

"Yes, of course, but—"

"Then we're on."

"I thought we were going to start this on Monday," moaned Amy. She fell back into the bed and begged, "Go away, Doctor, and let me sleep. Monday will come soon enough."

"Mom was up real late last night sewing," Dan provided.

"So sleep, Mom," Todd said with an amused laugh. "I'll

47

send the boys one at a time, and you can identify them. I'll band them and do some preliminary stuff while you get some shut-eye."

"Are you always this cheerful at the crack of dawn?" she groaned.

"Are you always this grouchy?" he countered with a completely entertained air. Amy launched a pillow. It sailed through the air and caught him in the chest. Four doughnut-filled mouths broke into raucous laughter behind him.

"You had better watch out for Mom when she's like this," a finally empty mouth declared. "She can hit anything all the way across the room."

"Jonathan Robert Wilkins—"

"Whoa! All three names! You are in for it now!" hooted one of the boys. All of them danced with mirth.

"I think I'm going to like working around here."

"You can like it from downstairs!" she grumbled from the bed.

"That's more than fair," he agreed. "I'm sorry. I figured since the boys were all up, you were, too. I didn't mean to awaken you or invade your bedroom."

"I'll see you downstairs in a minute." She then turned her attention to her sons and noticed the crumbs all over her hardwood floor. "Hey! I don't like food upstairs. You get those doughnuts into the kitchen this instant!" The kids made tracks immediately. Todd followed right behind.

She yanked on her jeans and a shirt, then ran a comb through her wild curls. The mirror reflected her scarlet cheeks and the glint in her eyes. "Be angry and sin not," she reminded herself as she hastened downstairs. Once there, she demanded, "Todd, what is your middle name?"

"Todd." His answer was quick and to the point.

"Your name is Todd Todd?" Kenny yelped with glee.

"No, buster. My middle name is Todd. I don't like my first name, so I use my middle name instead."

"So what is the first name?" Amy demanded, stomping toward him like a steam engine.

"Oooooh, you'd better head straight for the time-out chair," Mike suggested. "You have Mom really going now."

"Really?" Todd asked, squatting down and eyeing the boy with a smirk.

The boy nodded meaningfully.

"Your name?" Amy demanded one last time.

"What's in a name?" he avoided.

"Plenty. If my papers for the study consent are written up and signed by one Dr. Todd Avery, they are invalid."

"They all read 'Dr. A. Todd Avery', Mrs. Wilkins."

"And that A is for—" she fished.

"Avery," he evaded.

"No good," Dan broke in. " 'Fess up, Todd. When Mom is mad at you, she gets to use your real name. That's the rule."

"The rule?" Todd quirked his brow and looked at Amy in askance.

"House rule: Mom uses full names only in emergencies or when you're in big trouble."

"So what is your middle name, Amy?" Todd inquired with smooth evasion.

"Louise," supplied both of the younger twins beside him.

"Thanks, guys. Have another doughnut," Todd chuckled.

"Do you always play dirty?"

"Not at all. Amy Louise is a beautiful name for a lovely lady."

"Cut the garbage, Todd. Cough up what the 'A' stands for, or we don't play your game, do we, team?" Amy asked, raising her voice slightly.

Four boys suddenly agreed.

"Oh, boy, and you say I play dirty," Todd scolded. "What if I just tell your mom my name and make her promise to keep it a secret?"

"Come on, is that fair?" Ken and Dan cried out together.

Todd gave Amy a pleading look.

"Surely your name isn't that bad," she said softly.

"Worse," he rasped. "Just think of the hold you'd have over me if you were the only one who knew. . . ."

Amy tapped her chin playfully with one tapered finger.

"Guys, tell you what. I'll whisper it to Mom, and she'll decide. Fair enough?" The boys all groused, but finally agreed.

Amy grabbed him by the wrist and dragged him into her sewing room. Once there, she realized her hand couldn't even span his wrist's circumference. She gulped and let go, instantly aware of his size and power.

"Thanks, I owe you a big one," he whispered in a rumbling baritone that unsettled her even further.

Taking a step backward, Amy stammered, "I seem to need to keep score with you, Dr. A. Todd Avery."

To her horror, he shut the door quietly behind himself. "You know, I don't tell many people my name," he said softly.

Swallowing hard and trying desperately to keep control, Amy wrapped her arms around her ribs and choked out, "Is that so?"

"I should think I'd be the one to be nervous here," Todd remarked, taking in her defensive posture. He looked about the frilly sewing room. "Ah, but I've invaded your domain, haven't I?"

"Yes, you have."

"Then I'll confess my secret and leave rapidly, trusting you to be circumspect."

Amy nodded and worked to keep her breathing even. She could feel her palms growing sweaty.

"My first name is. . . ," he paused and gathered his nerve, "Antares."

"Antares?" she whispered back.

"Antares."

"You mean as in the biggest, brightest *red* star in the Scorpio constellation?" she confirmed with obvious disbelief.

A huge hand went up and patted the russet mop. "My father loved astronomy. The night I was born, he saw Antares perfectly; and then, there I was, big and red as could be. He had a crazy sense of humor and was sure the name was perfectly suited to me. Mom didn't even try to change his mind. She simply gave me a middle name that was fairly innocuous. Still, it's been difficult to live with."

"I suppose it has," Amy agreed.

"How do you know so much about Antares?"

"I haven't managed to go to college, but I take the tele-courses that are offered. I really enjoyed the astronomy series last year."

"You're full of surprises, aren't you, Amy Louise Wilkins?"

"Don't call me that, and I won't call you by yours," she bargained.

"I'm getting the better end of the deal. What's wrong with Louise?"

"Mom loved Louisa May Alcott's books. Come to find out, she was one of my father's distant relatives. My maiden name was Alcott. She twisted the middle name from May to Amy, then gave me Louise as a compromised middle name. Please do me a favor. Don't make any comments about me being a little woman. I'm in no mood to tolerate such non-sense today."

"That is a very reasonable request. You know, you can go back to bed for a while. I have plenty to do to keep busy."

Amy looked up at the ceiling. Her bed was right above

them. "Some things just aren't meant to be."

"Did you get to bed that late?" He inspected her more closely. Faint shadows showed under her eyes.

"Early," she corrected him. "Two-thirty, to be precise."

"And I came barreling in at six? You poor lady, you must be exhausted!"

"I needed to get some work done. I'll survive. I do this about twice a week. Now if you'll excuse me, I'd like to have a few minutes to pull myself together."

"Naturally." Todd took his cue and opened the door. She slipped past him and scampered upstairs.

The day went fairly well, all things considered. Amy needed to be reminded to wave her hand toward whomever she addressed. She was rigged up with a small, battery-operated bracelet with a laser wire extending down to a ring on each of her fingers. Todd had measured her fingers after the picnic, so the apparatus fit perfectly.

As he put it on her, he smiled. "You know, I was really worried about finding the right woman to wear this jewelry. I can see now that worry was wasted."

"This contraption feels funny."

"I'm sure it does. We only anticipated one set of twins, so the technicians had to add the second set of hardware. It's a bit more cumbersome than I hoped for, so I have them making another set for you that's lighter weight and scaled down. The new model should better suit your dainty wrist and small hand."

"Won't that be expensive?"

"We'll retool this one to fit me, but your comfort is key to the study. The university was more than willing to provide the new set." He helped her hook the clasp. "There. How's that?"

Amy rotated her hand and wiggled her fingers. "I suppose

I'll get used to it. It is rather scary looking."

"Let me show you how to operate the laser." Todd sat down next to her and tried to ignore her fresh scent. As he leaned closer, he realized the fragrance must have been from her shampoo. His shoulder brushed hers, and he noted how she immediately shifted away. He scooted in the opposite direction and said nothing. He needed to be able to touch her wrist and arm, but he didn't want her to feel crowded.

Each finger had a ring to indicate an individual boy. Todd suggested, "Why don't we go from oldest to youngest, Dan being the index finger and Mike being the pinkie?"

"Okay." She subtly turned one of the rings.

"You activate the rings by hitting the inside portion with the pad of your thumb. Once you do, you have three seconds to aim the outside laser stone on that ring and 'tag' the boy you've called by name." The laser operation took a little practice, but to Todd's delight, Amy soon got the hang of it.

Each of the boys wore armbands around their biceps. A laser tag appropriately aimed for their ID was counted internally, as were any incorrect ID. Todd moved the bands from their wrists to their upper arm after he realized that it was too difficult to tag the boys when they were facing away from Amy.

"The boys' bands are waterproof, so they can swim and bathe in them," Todd explained. "Your system is more sensitive, though. Casual hand washing is okay, but bathing and swimming will require you to remove it."

From his belt, Todd wore a series of small leather thongs lined with beads. Each bead represented an individual counter for motive. Each child had five thongs, each bearing a different color bead. Black beads indicated correction or reproof. Red was affection. The other three beads indicated attempts to fool anyone about identity. Yellow was for a capricious motive, brown to escape punishment, and orange to show anger as a motive. There was also a counter for when Amy called the children generically, as in "you boys" or "guys."

The boys all agreed not to mislead or fool their mother for the first day since she was trying to work the "jewelry" and it was difficult. By suppertime, Amy had the hang of it. She had only one problem: eating and addressing the children simultaneously was nigh unto impossible. With that problem coming to light, Todd swiftly grabbed her plate and cut all of her food into dainty bite-sized pieces. Then, he buttered her roll and slipped her napkin into her lap.

"I feel like a two-year-old!" Her cheeks flushed brightly as his fingers brushed her hip with the napkin.

"Not at all," he said in a husky voice. Neither of them was sure of the intent of his statement: Was he saying that she *shouldn't* feel like a two-year-old, or was he saying she did-n't *feel* like a two-year-old? Luckily, Dan spilled his milk and diverted their attentions.

"Dinner was one of the nicest meals I've had in ages," Todd stated after the boys were all tucked into their beds. "That veal was wonderful, and your boys were a scream when they talked about Davey Jackson's antics."

"Conversation is always lively. I'm never quite sure what will come out of their mouths. I feel like making one of those disclaimers, 'the views of the child are not necessarily those held by the parent'!"

Todd laughed heartily. "I have all sorts of crazy stories of the things kids have said to embarrass the daylights out of their parents. I figure that is part and parcel of the package you get upon delivery." He ran a scanner over the capsules he had retrieved from the boy's armbands. "Speaking of delivery, I need to ask you some basic background questions about your pregnancies and each of the boys. Do you mind giving me consent to obtain a copy of your medical records?"

"No! I mean yes! Oh, what I mean is, I'll tell you whatever is necessary." She wet her lips nervously and asserted, "Just give me a form, and I'll fill in the required information."

"You're pretty worn out, Amy. You only slept three-and-a-half hours last night. Why don't you just sign a few forms? I'll slog through the doctor's notes at my convenience."

Amy shuddered and crossed her arms around her torso. She knew the obstetrician had made notations regarding her bruises. She had lived in the battered women's shelter during her second pregnancy. That address would be on her chart as her place of residence. She wasn't ready for Todd to discover her past. She'd worked too hard to put it all behind her.

"No."

"No?" He looked up at her in obvious surprise.

"I made no bones about the fact that the invasion of our privacy concerned me greatly, Dr. Avery. Anything you wish to know needs to be put to me directly. I don't want you using other resources."

"Okay. You do realize I'll be careful to disguise identifying characteristics upon publication of my findings."

"I made certain you covered that provision in the consent. I even highlighted it."

"I noticed. Is there something specific I should know that you'd want to be omitted from general publication?"

"There is nothing I want you to know," she stated evasively, refusing to meet his gaze.

After a lengthy pause, Todd said quietly, "Amy, I'm going to level with you. I've worked in psychology for twelve years now. I'm pretty good at reading verbal and nonverbal messages. Something is bothering you right now, but I haven't the vaguest what I've said or done to upset you."

Leaping from the couch, Amy glowered at him. "*I* am not

to be scrutinized in this study, Dr. Avery. The simple fact of the matter is, you are here to quantitate whether I can tell which of my kids is which—that, *and nothing more*. I'd appreciate your keeping on task. Leave all of your other gobbledygook back at the office. If you can't, I'll put an end to all of this here and now!"

Todd kept a neutral expression and stated evenly, "Of course. Would you like to know how the scanners rated your accuracy today?"

His remarks knocked all of the wind out of her sails. Amy crumbled back onto the couch and nodded dumbly. She knew she'd overreacted. What he thought shouldn't matter, but for some reason, it did. Still, she couldn't make direct eye contact to read whatever expression lurked in his fathomless gray eyes.

"Mind you, the boys weren't trying to fool you and you were working the bugs out, but I'm really impressed."

Amy felt curious about the results, but she was also embarrassed by her outburst. She wished he would just leave. She sneaked a peek at him, and the baffled look on his face spoke volumes—but she couldn't help it. She had carefully constructed walls. Essential walls. They kept her from getting involved or hurt. . .and she wasn't about to let him crash through those walls. *Keep everything focused on the children*, her inner voice warned. Her vocal cords felt strained, and she choked out, "What did you find today?"

"Let's review one boy at a time. Dan was called by his name correctly twenty-four times and incorrectly once. A four percent error rate is on a par with what happens in families with singletons. Parents get distracted or rattled and call out any name."

"Yeah, I've seen that happen," Amy stated softly. She was twisting her fingers in her lap.

"Ken was called correctly nineteen times and incorrectly

twice. John was twenty-three and zip, and Mike was twenty-six and two. I'm impressed, Mrs. Wilkins."

She gave him a halfhearted smile.

"The discipline counters indicate that you nabbed each boy twice. I need to add beads for affection, because you topped off on all of them by the end of the day. I had eight beads for that, so I'm pretty amazed. The last fact scored was that you addressed them generically twelve times."

"So I use their names individually more often than I resort to gang mentality? I wondered and worried about that."

"I actually expected far more of that. In families with single-ton siblings, there is still a lot of the 'gang mentality' you're talking about. With four boys so close in age, I thought we'd see that as the rule rather than the exception."

"I suppose it still might be that way. Maybe because I'm wearing the band system I called them by their names more frequently than usual."

"Time will tell, though that may be a valid point."

"Thankfully, I only have two sets of twins. You'd never manage a study if I had three," Amy said as she looked down at the "jewelry."

"Did the weight of it bother you?"

She wrinkled her nose. "Not much. I'll probably forget it's even there by tomorrow. I'm not used to wearing bracelets."

"It's the latest in high-tech accessories," he teased.

"And to think that I tend to go for the old-fashioned stuff."

Todd chuckled as though she had told a fine joke. "You know," he said as he stopped laughing, "I'm the envy of all the researchers. They couldn't believe that you have two sets of identicals that are only eighteen months apart, nonrhyming names, and dressed differently. This study is already being earmarked as providing groundwork for several other studies we've had to abandon in the past."

"What does that mean?" Amy looked at him wearily. "Do you think I'll be content to zap my kids for the rest of their lives so that you can count how often they pick up their own socks?"

Todd chuckled again. "We actually did conduct one study about personality opposites—whether there was any truth to the good/bad twin, tidy/messy twin, bossy/pliant twin myths. The problem was, the researcher couldn't tell them apart well enough to collect sufficient data. The parents ended up going through an ugly divorce, and we backed out so that we didn't stress the kids any further. I'm positive that the study would benefit from your cooperation." He must have noticed her aghast expression because he hastened to add, "But first things first. We'll see if you can train me to tell them apart. After that, you can put an end to cooperating with any further programs if you find it too disruptive or distressing."

"Gee thanks," Amy replied wryly. "Maybe I ought to read the boys 'Romulus and Reemus' or some other twin myths if we get into this any deeper."

"Like the book you were doing at bedtime, huh? Do you always read to them at bedtime?"

"Yeah. We have Bible time, and then I read a chapter from a secular book. I think it's a good way to encourage them to read for themselves. I read to them each night if they've done their chores by seven forty-five. That way, I get them into bed at a decent time."

"You look like you should be heading for bed, too. Why don't I go over the guidelines for keeping the nighttime diary in case one of the boys gets up while I'm gone? Then, I'll leave."

"Okay."

Todd took out a journal and showed her the simple entry system. The process involved a basic checklist and code so she could make her record in a jiffy, then roll back over. Obviously, he'd put a lot of thought into developing such a tool. Amy said as much. "I can't ask you to open your home and your time to me and not try to simplify your work as much as possible, Amy. I'll try to make this as nonintrusive and easy on you as I can."

"Okay." She covered her mouth as she yawned.

"If eight-thirty is bedtime, what time do the boys usually get up, anyway?"

"Six o'clock. No matter how late they've been up or what the day of the week is, they're wide-awake at six. Blame it on Ken and Mike. Both of them have internal alarm clocks. The problem is, they wake up their brothers."

"This is going to be just about as bad as when I tracked sleep patterns of parents of newborn twins. No wonder you're yawning. I'll probably be doing the same if I don't get home and hit the hay, myself."

❧

Amy collapsed onto the edge of the bed. She started in on her bedtime prayers and fell asleep still wearing her jeans and T-shirt. By six the next morning, she was well rested, showered, and dressed in a pretty floral shirtwaist dress. The boys raced around in their pajamas as she made waffles for breakfast.

"Todd is here!" shouted one of the boys.

"Go ahead and let him in. Guys, you need to wash your hands. Breakfast is ready!"

"Good morning. Did you get any rest last night?" she asked as Todd entered the kitchen.

"A fair amount. You look like you got a good dose of rest." A smile lit his face. "I'm glad to see you already have the 'jewelry' on."

"Sure do. John, get the syrup out." She "zapped" the boy.

"Ken, you're in charge of orange juice." She zapped him as well.

"I'm Dan," the boy protested. "Orange juice isn't my job this week."

"Nice try, but I know better. Get the juice, dude," Amy shot back without batting an eye. "Todd, do you want some coffee?"

"Yeah, thanks. Okay, buddy. Time for truth. Which one are you?" Todd was standing by the orange juice monitor.

"I'm Kenny," he admitted with a grin. "You said we had to be good yesterday. Today, we thought we'd try to trick Mom."

Todd laughed and slid a yellow bead on Ken's thong for caprice.

Amy felt silly having Todd cut her waffle and bacon, but the boys were in top form, and she was laser zapping them right and left. Once, when she got up from the table to answer the phone, Ken and Dan acted as if they'd traded places when her back was turned. She wasn't fooled for a minute. Breakfast was half over before she realized Todd had sweetened her tea and even made her a second mug. "Whoops! We'll be late for church if we don't get moving. I'll put clothes out for you. Dan, you rinse off the dishes. Ken you put out the trash. Mike and John, go brush your teeth." A small burst of well-organized activity followed and soon everyone was ready to go.

Todd climbed into the van. "You know, I'm glad you drive a van. In a standard car, there wouldn't be a place for me to ride."

"That's true," Amy agreed. She pulled out of the driveway and glanced over at him. "Will you be coming to big church or to one of the Sunday school classes?"

"Are the boys in different classes?"

"Yes. Actually, we all start out together. After music and children's sermon, they filter on out to their own classes."

"Oh. I thought that was just something special last week because it was picnic day."

"No. It is the usual state of affairs, so name your poison. Kenny, stop making horns over Dan's head. John, stop kicking the back of Mom's seat!"

"How did you know about the horns?"

"I have eyes in the back of my head. They develop along with the bags under the eyes. You know, until I speak with the Sunday school teachers, it might be rather awkward for you to show up and monitor interactions."

"True. It's downright unethical. Maybe I could call them this week."

"Suit yourself."

They filed into church, and the boys remained with them for music, prayer, and general announcements. When it was time for Pastor Jordan to do the children's sermon, the boys went up to the altar and joined all of the other kids. Amy and Todd were left in the pew together. He was a few spaces away, yet she still withdrew slightly.

Her avoidance was subtle; but she hoped Todd took note and understood. Here she was, a widow with a strange man who invaded her home from early morning to late evening seven days a week. It would be important for them to be circumspect. Society would breathe down their necks, and every busybody in the community would be staring and gossiping. That might not bother Todd a bit, but Amy knew she and the boys would bear the brunt of any chatter or rumors. She resolved to be extraordinarily cautious.

❧

"I'd like for you guys to play some games for me, if you don't mind," Todd ventured the next morning. He needed to administer several of the personality profile exams and see if there were minor differences between the kids. Amy had okayed the test earlier.

"Okay," Mike agreed. "Can we make you a deal? We play your games if you'll show us how to bat like you did at the picnic."

"Now there's a good idea. I didn't know if you boys were sports fans or not."

Amy merely laughed at the outrageous statement. "Todd, my boys should have been born wearing gym trunks."

As they cleared away the breakfast dishes, Todd said, "I need you to fill out several surveys on how you perceived each boy. The questions will become repetitive by the fourth time through, so feel free to take breaks." He noted how she took him at his word. Every once in a while, she'd wander through the kitchen and dining room to watch what he did with the boys. Todd had them piecing together wooden puzzles, tape-recording stories about pictures, cutting shapes and patterns out of a book, completing sentences, and doing a variety of things such as skipping and hopping.

"You make one whale of a baby-sitter," she teased.

"I'm nowhere near your league, lady. You are on-duty twenty-four hours a day, every day, all year long. And you do it all alone."

Amy cleared her throat and excused herself. From the kitchen table, he watched as she sat back down in the living room and picked up one of the surveys. Her hand shook.

"Amy?" Todd stood by the coffee table and gave her a second. She looked rattled. "The boys are busy." He sat down and leaned forward. In a muted voice, he said, "That's the second time I walked into an emotional minefield. I don't want to spend the entire summer hitting your raw nerves. Is it the fact that you are doing it alone, or was it your husband?"

"I prefer being alone with the boys, Dr. Avery." Her tone was decidedly icy. "The boys have no memory of their father, and I don't wish to discuss him."

"Other than basic medical and ethnic information for the younger set, that will be easy enough. The same information transfers to Ken and Dan easily; but since their father was around for their first year of life, I'd like a little more information."

Todd had noticed that there were no pictures of Mr. Wilkins around the house. Strange. Eerie, as a matter of fact. The boys never spoke of him, either.

"I'm done!"

"John. (Zap.) Why don't you get Mom some lemonade, please. Would you care for any, Dr.—Todd?"

"Yes, thank you." Amy was obviously distressed and wanted John away from the discussion. "We can talk about all this after the boys are in bed tonight," he offered.

Amy merely nodded and pored over the survey on the clipboard. Todd noted her trembling hand. The vivacious, sunny face he enjoyed watching had become alarmingly pale and pinched. As he turned to leave the room, he heard her pencil snap in half.

five

Todd kept a running list of the names Amy used for her boys. She referred to them by their given names and diminutives; their full names when they were in trouble and generics: you guys, you boys, team, folks, dudes, monsters. She also drew from a wealth of affectionate terms: buddy, moppet, pumpkin, sport, little man, slugger, honey, sweetie, munchkin. The list went on and grew almost hourly.

After a productive morning, Todd announced an end to the testing. A picnic of peanut butter and jelly sandwiches, chips, carrot sticks, apple boats, and milk was held under the awning in the backyard. A slight breeze ruffled everyone's hair and refreshed them.

"Guys, I want to ask you a favor," Todd stated in a relaxed drawl. "Sometimes I'm going to try to guess which kid you are. If I'm wrong, please forgive me. I need to get a feel for how often I'm right or wrong before your mom tries to teach me how to identify you. What I need from you is absolute honesty. You can play any of the usual ploys and tricks you want; but if I call you by name, I need you to be dead-level honest with me if I'm right or wrong. Can I count on you?" He spoke man-to-men without condescension. He looked them straight in the eye and said his piece.

"If we agree, will you be able to teach the school how to tell us apart?" Ken asked hopefully.

"I can't make any promises, Ken. You are Ken, aren't you?" A nod made Todd beam. "The fact of the matter is, we're all like detectives. We're trying to unravel a mystery

64

and I don't know if we can do it or not. If we don't, we'll have a fun summer together. If we do, your lives may become a whole lot simpler. I won't lie to you. I'm just not sure what is going to happen."

"I'll do it," Ken stated.

A trio of "me toos" followed.

"Thanks, guys. Are you ready for some batting practice?"

Even with the boys playing stunts and wearing identical clothing, Amy was still accurate about them well over eighty percent of the time. Her accuracy dropped when they were a fair distance away, a fact Todd felt deserved further scrutiny. Dinner was done, the next chapter of the book read, and the boys all snugly tucked away in bed.

By an unspoken agreement, Todd and Amy met in the living room each night for a recap. Todd pulled out a check and handed it to Amy.

"What is this?"

"I'm given a food allowance when I work on-site like this. Actually, I've never eaten so well. I thought you might want to deposit this check to help defray the cost of my enormous appetite. I'll get the same amount each month, if that helps you with your planning."

"Oh." She gave him a surprised look.

"Surely you didn't think I'd eat like a host of termites and not help out!"

"I hadn't given the matter any thought."

"Believe me," he smiled, "by the time we hit the grocery store again, you will."

"Maybe you ought to make up a list of food preferences and dislikes for me."

"I'll eat anything but liver and brussels sprouts. Is that too picky?"

"Not at all. I don't think the boys have ever had either. I

hate them both, too," she giggled in confession.

"Well, at least we agree. I'll start compiling personality profiles on the boys and compare the test results with your perceptions when I get home tonight. Do you want me to share the results with you, or do you want to have me keep them sealed for a while?"

"I'd rather not know. I don't want to get so wound up in all of the particulars that I don't simply enjoy having them all home for the summer. Does that sound too ridiculous?"

"Not at all. Actually, I think keeping the study is best served by protecting the results. If I change the way you perceive their personalities, you might alter the way you identify them."

"I can see how that might happen," she agreed.

"Amy, we need to work through some difficult issues tonight. I need to get some family and medical history from you." Todd saw her stiffen immediately. "I'll try to make this as painless as possible.

"Can't I just fill out a form for you or something?"

"I have one here that will give me particulars about the genetic pool and the boy's general health. I need to have you fill it out. There's another form about their father's medical background, ethnicity, personality traits, etc., and one for you, as well. The questionnaire asks all of the usual questions and traces the pregnancies. Do you have all of that information?"

"Yes." She stared at her lap and clenched her hands into chalk white lumps.

"Good," he soothed. "That is the bulk of it. There are a few things for which I don't have a form. Basically, I need to know about how your husband interacted with Dan and Ken. They were almost a year and a half old when he died, so even though they don't remember him, he undoubtedly made an impact on them in many ways."

"No! No, he hasn't. I mean, he didn't." Amy looked positively frantic.

"Amy, I'm sorry if this is a painful subject."

"Forget the apologies, Todd. I'm not interested in being pacified. My husband saw the boys as proof of his virility and nothing more. He was a trucker and was gone the lion's portion of the time. We were separated just after the twin's first birthday. I have nothing else to say. That subject is off limits."

Agitated was a polite term for her state of mind. Viewing her with a keen clinical eye, Todd realized Amy was nearly panic-stricken. There was a wealth of information under a very tumultuous relationship there. If things were that rocky, why in the world did she get pregnant again? For a mother of twins to conceive again so soon was highly unusual. Most of them were so swamped that they were very leery of having another baby for quite a time, if ever again at all. As for them being separated—she seemed to be a woman of abiding commitments. Had her husband betrayed her and left her behind? Even while she was pregnant? That would explain why she was so emotionally fragile. Pity surged through him.

"I won't press you, Amy. I told you earlier that I'm not in this to make things hard on you. Why don't I let you start filling out the forms while I do some of the scans and look at some of the tests from this morning?"

"Whatever." Amy accepted the forms and started filling them out. By the time Todd left, she had almost completed them.

He took the papers back to his mother's house and looked through them with interest. The boys were in good health and always had been. Both sets of twins were born at thirty-six weeks gestation, meaning they were four weeks early. Statistically, twins were usually about three weeks early, so their gestation was right on par with what Todd had expected.

Birth weights had been in the high four-pound range for the first pair, and they were bottle-fed a soy milk formula. The birth weights for the second pair were in the mid-six-pound range and they were breast-fed exclusively until six months, when baby foods were introduced. The comparison was startling. He wondered why the differences. The most obvious factor was that the father was absent for the last portion of the second pregnancy and dead just before the birth. How much did that figure in? How did it factor in at all?

Todd scanned Amy's personal form. She was discreet with her information, but she didn't sugarcoat it, either. She was barely nineteen when she gave birth the first time, twenty the second time. Both deliveries were done by cesarean section. Amy hadn't listed the reasons why. That was fairly common, especially if the lower twin wasn't head down, so Todd gave it little thought. Amy's forms indicated that her mother was deceased. She had died when Amy was fifteen. The next line showed her father was also deceased. He had died only three years ago, and the cause was listed as alcoholism. Amy, herself, was healthy. The area on surgeries was all crossed off as negative other than the births. The area on accidents, broken bones, and sundry other issues was curiously blank. It was on the back of the form, at the bottom. She may have thought it unimportant and just moved on. He had given her an awful lot to fill out.

Todd grabbed the sheet on the father's history. Joseph Randall Wilkins. Caucasian. Age: deceased. Date of birth: Todd did some quick math. Comparing the forms, he determined the father was twenty-five when the older boys were born. He was a good-sized guy—five eleven and a half, one hundred and ninety-two pounds. Brown hair, hazel eyes. Family medical history was completely unremarkable. Amy had been sparing in what she put down. Occupation: trucker.

Drank alcohol. Did not smoke.

The form asked for an estimate of the amount of time spent by the father with the children during the first year of life. It had an example of 365 days multiplied by two hours each day to give a total of 730 hours spent as what a sample father had for his involvement. Amy gave everything away in that one last box. 23 days. Five minutes. Total: 115 minutes. Five minutes shy of two hours' total for a whole year. No wonder she was so sensitive.

Her life in those days must have been a nightmare: nineteen, twins, recovering from a cesarean, no mother, her father alcoholic, so he was of no help. And Mr. Big Trucker had deigned to give her a whopping two hours of help for the whole year. Add to that, the fact that she was already carrying another set of twins.

Todd decided Amy had every right to be defensive and guarded about the issue. His questioning put her in a precarious spot. She shouldn't have to lie to her sons about their father. Neither should she have to speak ill of the dead. Especially the father of her children. Whenever he brought the issue up, he put her in an impossible situation. The wounds were still present. When had she had time to work out the issues? If the boys were happily oblivious, perhaps things were best left that way. She had been absolutely clear tonight: Say nothing more. He would comply with her demand.

The next three weeks were a blur. The Wilkins boys were dynamos from sunup to eight-thirty each night. There were games of soccer, baseball, basketball, badminton, and croquet. What they lacked in skill, they made up for in enthusiasm. They flew Frisbees, went swimming at Todd's mother's backyard pool, went on picnics and to movie matinees, bowled, and played miniature golf. Through it all, the zap of Amy's laser was ever present.

Todd marveled at how Amy decided on what to do for the day. There were several days when she threw the boys out into the monstrous-sized backyard and told them to "have at it." On those days, a good half dozen other youngsters appeared as if by magic. The invading army of neighborhood kids didn't even phase Amy. Her philosophy—as long as there was lemonade to drink, toilet paper in the downstairs bathroom, and nobody was bleeding, life was great.

A box of adhesive bandages, Bactine, and cotton balls sat in a drawer by the kitchen sink. All of the children knew that simple fact and often doctored themselves for the small scrapes. Amy insisted they report and let her inspect any "ouchies," but then encouraged independent care. "Otherwise, I'd take up full-time nursing," she had explained with a silvery peal of laughter.

At least twice a week, she packed a fair-sized cooler with a lunch and they took off on adventures: a hike, a park, and weekly jaunts to the library or the skating rink.

Amy was never shy about joining in and playing with her sons. She shot hoops, ran races, miniature golfed, bowled, and skated. Todd was worn out keeping up with her. He wondered how she managed to stay up late to monogram cheerleading outfits for the local high school, baseball teams, custom-made shirts for local physicians and moguls. There were days when she was obviously tired, but she kept right on going.

They all enjoyed riding bikes and quite often traveled fair distances. Amy had warned Todd, so he brought over his own bike. Once a week, she would let the boys ride up and down the street while she edged and mowed the lawn. Other days, when she would weed the flowerbed, Amy allowed them to ride or skateboard as well.

"Amy," Todd exclaimed in amazement. "You do the gardening?! You look too small to push that lawn mower!"

Seeing her bristle, he backpedaled, "I mean, the lawn is huge, and the kids are too young to do this. I just figured you hired someone to handle this chore."

She shot him a "you-male-chauvinist" look and threw her weight against the lawn mower to move it. The sight of her pushing it out of the garage made his jaw drop.

"Isn't that your phone?"

Amy stood still for a second, then winced as she glanced down the block toward the boys.

"I'll keep an eye on them. Go ahead." As soon as she went inside, Todd started cutting the grass. When she came back out, he refused to turn the mower over to her, claiming that to do so outraged his sense of chivalry. Thereafter, they came to a compromise whereby Amy would edge and sweep as Todd mowed.

Todd noticed something rather unique about Amy's sons. They rarely got physically nasty with one another. Sure, the boys called each other names—harmless ones that Amy still disapproved of—doofus, klutz, nitwit. He was more accustomed to denigrating and often unprintable names being bandied about. Since twins almost always shared the same room (and often even the same bed) there was a matter of lashing out for space that Todd had come to expect as normal. Verbal and physical assault were part and parcel of coping, as far as Todd could determine. For four boys to share toys, clothes, rooms and vie for a single parent's attention, it was strange that almost all of the fights stayed within the verbal arena.

One day when Davey Jackson and another boy were over playing in the backyard, a fight erupted. Both boys threw punches, and Amy stepped in at once. She insisted the boys sit across the picnic table, resolve their differences, then sent them each to their own homes.

"Whoa. Mom really showed them, didn't she?" Kenny whispered to Todd.

"What makes you say that?" he countered with an open-ended question. He was hoping Ken would give him more information.

"Mom doesn't let us hit—"

"Ever!" Dan finished the sentence with a sage nod of his dark, curly head.

"Never?" Todd clarified.

"We get in time-out for a long, long—"

"—long, long, long time if we punch," Dan finished again.

"Really?"

"Yep. Mom says if you can't solve a problem by talking it out, then you'd better just walk away." Daniel was on a roll.

"Beating each other up only makes things worse," Ken inserted as if by rote.

"So do you guys fight when Mom isn't watching?" Todd asked quietly. He knew Amy couldn't hear them.

Both looked terribly guilty. They shot looks at one another and over in their mother's direction. "Sometimes," admitted Kenny in a hushed whisper.

"But we don't let her know. She goes way crazy if she sees us hitting. We feel bad when we slug each other, too. We even ask Jesus to forgive us. Don't tell her!" Dan begged.

"Way crazy? What does that mean?"

"She cries and makes us do time-out and takes away privileges."

"Way crazy," Todd agreed. "The past is the past, but I want you to know I agree with your mom, so don't expect me to approve of any fighting. Since Jesus forgave you and you've decided to behave, I'll keep my lips sealed." He made a show of making a zippered motion across his mouth.

Later that night, Todd pondered over the whole matter. He

realized Amy had never once used corporal punishment. By no means was she a lenient parent, though. For a woman to live with four boys who would certainly tower over her in the not-so-distant future, she was wise to have stringent rules and enforce them at this stage. Nonviolence was reasonable. The behavior beads were counting up to a level that clearly indicated she brooked no sass, but the affection beads always outnumbered the discipline by a wide margin. Obviously, Amy didn't get "way crazy" very often.

Todd noted with interest that Amy held the neighbors' kids to the same level of accountability as her own sons. He wondered if that stemmed from familiarity, or if she was that way with all kids. He soon had a golden opportunity to see her with several other children.

The church planned its annual vacation Bible school, and Amy volunteered to help run the program. She was deep in preparation and had enlisted her sons to try the crafts and see if they were practical and fun. She cut out figures for the flannel board to tell the story and baked cookies for the snacks. Everything went off without a hitch.

He enjoyed watching Amy work with the children. She was obviously gifted with them. Vacation Bible school also gave Todd an opportunity to watch the twins interact with several other children in an enclosed area and a structured setting. He gained a fair notion of what their behavior was like in the classroom.

As time went by, he started to detect intriguing behavior patterns. Unfortunately, they didn't help him pinpoint any techniques to identify the boys on an individual basis. He felt a bit discouraged, but the daily joy of being with Amy and the boys made him more determined to discover a way to tell the boys apart.

Todd enjoyed going to VBS for several reasons. On the

very last day, he confessed, "This has been fun—almost like stepping back in history to my own childhood."

"Sometimes people try to make their faith too complicated." Amy smiled as she took the flannel board off of the easel. "Christ said, 'Suffer the children to come unto me, for such is the kingdom of heaven.' As adults, I think we try to get bogged down in works and worries instead of living by faith and grace."

Todd looked at her, then carefully arranged the Bible verse cards in a stack. He started to read them aloud. " 'For all have sinned and come short of the glory of God'. . . . 'For God so loved the world, that He gave His only Son, that anyone who believes in him will not die, but have eternal life'. . . ." He glanced up. "I remember the old King James 'begotten Son' and 'whosoever' and 'everlasting'."

Amy smiled, then softly said, "The words are just as true now as they were when they were first given by God or when they were put into the King James English."

The kids were all out on the playground, and the church was peaceful. A shaft of sunlight illuminated the cross on the wall. Todd stared at it and nodded. In a pensive voice, he said, "Those words are as true now as they were when I gave my heart to Christ many years ago."

"Are you still walking with Christ, Todd?" she asked in a near whisper. "Is He truly your Lord?"

He slowly turned to face her. "No. I've fallen away."

They held each other's gaze. Amy wet her lips, then asked, "Is that what you want?"

He slowly shook his head. "Not anymore. Seeing how you and the boys live each day for Christ; listening to the pastor each week. . .I realize what I've been missing. I want that peace and assurance."

"The altar is always open," she invited.

Todd knelt at the wooden railing and held out his hand. "Please, pray with me. I'm not very good at finding the right words to say."

"You don't have to be eloquent," she said as she settled near him. "Christ knows the intent of our hearts and opens His arms in welcome."

He looked back up at the cross. "Time for this prodigal son to come home."

☙

The Saturday after vacation Bible school was over, Amy accepted Todd's invitation to bring the boys over to his mom's place for swimming and a barbecue. Amy had diligently taught the boys to swim before they turned four. Now, they were wild in the water. She sat at the poolside and zapped away, mindful to not get the "jewelry" wet. Her percentage level of accuracy on identifying the boys remained in the high eighties. It didn't matter if they were wet or dry.

Zap. "Ken, let go of your brother. John—" Zap. "He doesn't appreciate being thrown around like that." "Pssst. Dan." Zap. "John." Zap. "Sneak over and push Todd into the water."

They dragged Todd into the water and dunked him several times. He wrestled with the boys with joyous abandon and finally pulled himself out. He was huge and wet and vaguely threatening when he sauntered over toward Amy. She pretended not to notice him, calling out to Mike not to run on the wet concrete and zapping him. Todd came so close, he blocked out the sun. Deciding to give up and look at him, Amy craned her head back until it hit the metal edge of the pool chair.

"Take off the jewelry, Amy," Todd ordered in a playful threat.

"Nothing doing. It's my insurance policy that you hooligans leave me my peace."

"Take it off."

"Not a chance. Where do you get off rapping out commands, anyway?"

"It is a throwback. Genetic, I'm sure."

"Oh, I see. Barbarosa?"

"Is *that* his name? *Barbara Rosa!*" Mike exploded loudly. All four of the boys stared at Todd with undisguised shock, then fell into unrestrained laughter.

"Now look what you've done!" he thundered at Amy. He leaned over and swiftly divested her of the laser mechanism. "You're going to pay for that!" Amy let out a terrified screech as Todd bodily lifted and threw her over his shoulder. He strode over to the pool and ignored Amy's rigidity and gasps. With negligent ease, he tossed her straight into the deep end.

Everyone cannonballed in on top of her.

The episode alarmed Amy tremendously. Todd was mad at her. He was big and strong and had easily lifted, carried, and thrown her. The scene was a replay of several bouts with Joseph. When she first surfaced, everyone was laughing at her spluttering. A few minutes passed before John asked in amazed disbelief, "Are you crying? Hey! Mom is crying!"

"Amy?" Todd stood so close he blocked out the sun again. She'd retreated to the shallow end of the pool and now quailed away. "You guys go swim at the other end of the pool. Amy, are you okay?" His hand closed loosely around her forearm.

He didn't sound angry anymore. Amy had developed a sixth sense about the undercurrent of rage, and she wasn't picking up on any feelings of anger now. She let out a choppy sigh and backed away.

Dan paddled over. "I landed right on top of her head when I jumped in. Are you okay, Mom?"

"I'm okay." Her lie sounded weak, she thought.

"Where?" Todd lifted his hand to her head, and she flinched. "Don't be afraid, Amy. I'll be gentle. Where did he bump you?" Fingers threaded through her short, wet curls, mapping the shape of her skull with surprising tenderness.

Joseph was like that, too. Suddenly contrite and attentive after the fireworks were over. Sometimes he'd brought her flowers after he'd beaten her the night before. Always, he said that he had beaten her for the last time, that he loved her, that he would never do it again. . . .

"Really, I'm fine. I think I'll just get out." Amy pushed away before he could complete his examination and discover there was no lump. She slipped out of the pool and immediately dried off. As soon as she wasn't drenched, she donned the laser jewelry again. To her way of thinking, the equipment provided her with a modicum of safety.

Todd stood waist deep in the pool and looked at Amy with puzzlement. He turned around when John splashed him and invited, "Let's play Marco Polo!"

He cast a glance back at Amy. "Are you all right?"

She twitched a brave smile and nodded. His look made it clear he wasn't convinced, but he turned back to the boys.

For the next half-hour, Amy stayed exceptionally quiet. When something needed to be said, she rasped out orders, but she no longer called any of the boys by name. The laser tag hadn't registered once since she'd gotten out of the pool. She felt nearly paralyzed with fear.

"Hey, all of you men! Listen up. It looks to me like your mom ended up with a royal headache. You kids splash around a bit, but keep your noise to a dull roar. I'll torch the burgers while she rests. Plan?"

"Plan!" they all agreed. He took care of setting everything on the picnic table, then called everyone over. For the first time, he announced, "I think today it is my turn to pray."

Amy said nothing, but bowed her head.

"Heavenly Father, thank You for bringing us together and

for taking care of our needs. Bless this food, and I pray that You'd especially touch Amy so she'll feel better. In Jesus' name, amen."

The boys dug in with gusto. Amy barely nibbled at the edge of her burger. "Is my cooking that bad?" Todd asked a short while later, surveying Amy's virtually untouched plate.

She pulled her swimsuit cover-up a little tighter. "I'm sorry. I'm just not very hungry."

"I think we ought to try something." Amy gave him a wary look. "We need to get a baseline statistic for how often I correctly and incorrectly identify the boys. Why don't we have me wear the jewelry for the evening? I'll drive us back to your place, read, and tuck the boys in bed. In three hours, we'll have a fair idea about my track record."

"But—"

"But nothing. You stayed up late last night sewing, and you're bushed. Now you cracked your head and are feeling miserable. When we get to your place, you're hitting the sack."

Amy wavered. An internal warning signal told her not to challenge him and invite more anger. The other voice inside her head demanded that she be responsible for the boys. If Todd could be violent with her, her sons weren't safe with him, either.

A warm hand cupped her cheek. "I'll take your silence for assent, Amy. I'm sorry you got hurt. The rough-housing was my fault. I shouldn't have started all of the horseplay. A small woman like you needs to be protected from all of that kind of rough stuff."

She closed her eyes to hold back the tears.

❧

Later that night, Amy curled up in her bed and blinked slowly at the streetlight shining through the slatted shade. Todd had just left. She was too worried about the boys to leave them in his care. She'd opted to make a show of taking some aspirin and coiled up like a cat on the couch, sipping tea until Todd was ready to leave.

Todd had done a remarkable job with the boys. After they all bathed, they sat spellbound as he read to them. He'd made sure to read from the Bible first, then he took the other book Amy read each night and did a chapter from it, too. He even put inflection in his voice while he retold the saga of what befell the pioneering Ingallses. Tolerating no argument, he made sure all four sets of teeth were brushed and that everyone had a last drink of water before he declared "lights out." All of those evenings of observations had supplied him with a sufficient battle plan.

"You're next, lady." He'd scowled at her as he stood next to the couch. "I hate the way you look, all pale and tired. How's the head?"

"I took aspirin."

"I'm not convinced they've done you much good. Go on upstairs, and I'll compile today's data at my place. I'm going to take your keys so I can lock up behind me, Amy, so don't be looking for them."

"My keys!" She was aghast. He would have access to their home and the van—she wouldn't be able to get the boys away from him if he had the keys! She bolted upright and instantly paid the price for moving too swiftly on an empty stomach. Her dizziness made her melt back down onto the couch.

Muttering under his breath, Todd picked her up and mounted the stairs. "You can sleep in what you have on," he decided aloud, staring at the jersey knit short outfit she wore. He laid her on the bed and covered her with a light quilt. "I'll be certain to lock the door, so don't worry about that. Tomorrow morning, I'll let myself in if the boys aren't up yet. And I'm taking care of breakfast. For once in your motherhood, you are sleeping in!"

Amy remained on the bed, rigid and speechless. She heard Todd wander down the hallway, peeking in on the boys one last time. His footfall on each stair announced his descent, and the keys in the lock rattled loudly enough to let Amy know everything was secured. The hum of his Corvette's engine grew dim as Todd rounded the corner and drove off.

Amy lay there and replayed the afternoon over and over again. "Horseplay," he'd called it. Was that all the incident amounted to? Harmless, lighthearted horseplay? The boys certainly thought so. Had she overreacted? Was Maise right? Were all men *not* like Joseph had been? Certainly, Joseph would have never gone through the protracted bedtime rituals with four rowdy boys. Joseph would have left her down on the couch, if not the floor, after calling her vile names and abusing her. Todd tended the boys well and even tucked her in carefully, leaving them all safe. She huddled under the covers and couldn't believe that she remained unharmed. In addition, Todd had prayed for the first time—and he'd prayed specifically for her. There was too much to think about.

As she lay there, she felt as if the Holy Spirit were whispering to her, "Trust Me to protect you." Guilt washed over her. She'd let her worries take over instead of committing her fears to the Lord. She prayed for forgiveness and cried herself to sleep.

six

Muffled noises and the smell of bacon teased the edges of Amy's consciousness. She nestled deeper into the mattress and ignored the signs of morning. Surely, she was dreaming. The digital display on her alarm clock read eight o'clock. Eight o'clock! How could that be! She scurried out of bed and poked her head out of the door just in time to see Todd precariously balancing a tray as he and the boys climbed the stairs.

"Go back to bed, Mom."

"We're bringing you breakfast in bed!"

"Oh, wow!" she laughed.

"You heard the troops, Amy. Don't spoil the fun. Climb onto the bed so this labor of love will be official." Todd gave her a quirky grin.

Getting into the spirit of the fun, Amy pulled her robe on over her shorts and sat with her back to the headboard. Out of habit, she reached over to her nightstand to get the laser system.

"Here's your laser, Mom. Todd was wearing it last night and had left it downstairs."

Amy activated the system as she donned the device. Zap. "Thanks, Daniel. This smells great, guys!"

"Todd says that breakfast is the only meal he knows how to cook," John tattled.

"I made the toast," Mike boasted.

"And a fine job you did, moppet. Are you going to taste test it for me?" Amy held out the slightly burned square for the boy to nibble. Crumbs fell everywhere. True to form, everyone took a bite, even though the toast remained in Amy's hand.

"Barbara Rosa didn't get a bite," Ken needled.

Amy's eyes widened as Todd came close. He steadied her suddenly quavering hand with his and stared directly into her eyes as he took a bite. He didn't let go. "I'll eat the rest of this if you don't tell them that my name isn't Barbara Rosa," he threatened softly.

His gray eyes were dancing. *He really isn't angry with me,* Amy thought to herself. The realization rocked her. His full lips parted, and he took another bite. His mustache brushed her fingertips and tickled. Amy knew she should say something or move, but she was frozen.

"He really is going to eat all your toast!" Dan gasped as Todd took the next bite. The boys all hooted in gleeful disbelief as Todd finished the small last bite and licked Amy's fingers. His eyes were still trained on her, and she felt the tingling of a blush creep up to heat her cheeks.

"Are you going to tell them that Barbara Rosa isn't my name, or do I eat the bacon next?" he asked in an amused tone that was so husky, Amy gulped.

"The eggs are getting cold," she objected halfheartedly.

"Okay, I'll eat the eggs first, then the bacon if you don't salvage my reputation. I'll be ruined if you let them carry on this ridiculous notion." His voice crackled with mirth.

Amy reclaimed her hand at long last with a merry trill. "Oh, all right. Listen here, my gang. Todd's real name isn't Barbara Rosa." She accepted her fork from Todd with a tilt of her head in thanks.

"Then why did you call him that?" groused Ken. "I thought that name was really funny."

"I thought it was funny, too, Kenny." Zap. "But you misunderstood me. I was calling him Barbarosa—after the pirate who was also called Red Beard."

"A pirate?"

"Named Red Beard?"

"But Todd doesn't have a beard—"

"Only a mustache!"

"Tell you what, guys. We'll go to the library today and find something to read about the scoundrel named Red Beard. Would you like that?"

Her suggestion was met with enthusiasm. She finished her breakfast and thanked "all of the men in my life" for the meal, then shooed them out so she could hop into the shower.

"How did you fare on IDing the boys yesterday?" Amy inquired as they sat in the shade of a large tree. The trip to the library had been a success. Having located and read a few snippets about Barbarosa, the boys were suitably impressed. They stopped by the grocery store and got a box of ice cream sandwiches as a treat. Everyone had one, and she and Todd sat in the shade as the boys ran off their considerable energy in the park.

Todd groaned theatrically.

Zap. "Ken!" Zap. "John! Not so high on the swings and no jumping off!" Amy bellowed. She turned to Todd. "Sorry."

"Think nothing of it. I managed to prove the law of averages."

"Fifty-fifty?" Amy clarified.

"Precisely. Whoa! Hey! Look at Dan on the bar!"

Looking over at her son, Amy laughed. "Isn't he something? He got first place last year in our backyard Olympics for the bars."

"Backyard Olympics?"

"Yeah. We've held them for the past two years, and they were such a hit that we'll be doing them again next week. Somehow or other, I'd assumed the boys had told you all about the games."

"Not a word."

"Fifteen more minutes, guys!" she called out after glancing at her watch. "Basically, we have kid-style games and competition. Who can do the most sit-ups or somersaults in three minutes, the longest period of standing on your head, speed skipping, the most flips on the bar, that kind of entertainment. I hang up five hula hoops in a facsimile of the Olympic sign and the children earn ribbons."

"You're serious about this, aren't you?"

"Why wouldn't I be? The kids love it."

"Amy Wilkins, of all of the homes I've been in, observed, and delved through, yours has to be the most novel, fun, and interesting."

"Wow. Thanks. I think that's because I have such terrific little guys helping me out. They're what life is all about."

"You have that all turned around. They are terrific only because you are their mother."

She shook her head. "No, Todd. We all love one another because God put us together and fosters a special love in our home."

He nodded without a moment's hesitation. "The spiritual strength in your home is foundational. I won't deny that. Still, a mother is the heart of the home. You certainly have the most loving and tender heart of any mom I've seen."

Flushing brightly, Amy demurred, "That is very high praise, but I'm sure your own mother—"

"Happily stopped after one child and spent most of her days doting on her absentminded husband and worrying about how to keep that one son quiet."

"Oh, no!"

"I'm afraid so. She's after me now to make her a grand-mother, and I have this funny feeling she'll actually be a terrific one. Time and age have changed her in admirable ways.

She now travels and volunteers at a preschool and does all sorts of interesting projects, but that came about after Dad died. She was always very compassionate, but she never did much along the fun or creative line. Certainly not backyard Olympics! And I *never* saw her in a swimsuit—even though we have a pool!"

"Why didn't you say so? I would have never gone over there in my—"

"That is exactly why I didn't say anything! A mother *should* play and swim and romp with her kids. I'm putting you on warning here and now: If you try to sneak over there the next time without your suit, I'll throw you in—clothes and all."

"You wouldn't!"

"Want to try me?" His jaw was thrust forward pugnaciously, and he had a strange look in his eye. Amy wasn't at all sure he wasn't dead-level serious.

Amy made a spluttering noise.

He leaned toward her and asked in an undeniably husky baritone, "Are you thinking it over? Your unassuming one-piece swimsuit versus a sopping wet, clinging shorts set. That would be a fine sight. You're a lovely woman—one any man should appreciate."

Amy jumped up as if she were sitting on hot coals. This conversation was rapidly sliding toward flirtation, and she wanted nothing to do with that. "Okay boys! Head 'em up and move 'em out!"

The boys gathered up at her call, and Mike asked, "Gee Mom, why are you so red?"

"Am I?" Amy asked, pressing a hand to her warm cheek self-consciously. "I guess it was hotter out here than I thought."

"Indeed. You could certainly say that," Todd oozed meaningfully. His smirk irritated Amy to no end, and she shot him a nasty look. He merely laughed in response.

In a small corner of her heart, the idea thrilled her that Todd felt playful toward her. Did he find her appealing? No. That was too scary. Never again. She had vowed that she would never again be involved with a man. Once had been enough for an entire lifetime. Dr. Avery could just keep focused on his study.

ða

When Todd arrived the next day, Amy was already doing laundry. Todd eyed the wet clothes and turned away. He fought grinning at her, knowing she'd be mortified after yesterday's exchange. He knew situations like this one made her rue that she had ever agreed to the study. His intrusion into her home at times like this undoubtedly galled her. She was a woman who cherished her privacy. She looked more than grateful when the phone rang as she began to fold clothes.

With the boys out in the backyard practicing for the Olympics, Amy neatly creased shirts and jeans into orderly forms and stacked them into color-coded baskets. The boys were responsible for putting their own clothes away. With the speaker phone button depressed, she was able to talk and have her hands free. Dr. Garvey had given her number to a mom with newborn twins. The woman called in needed advice and support.

Todd sat and openly eavesdropped on the conversation. Amy had shrugged her consent when he raised his brows in inquiry, and then politely asked the new mother if she minded him listening in. The tearful woman gave consent without wasting a second, so he didn't feel out of line doing so. He was interested in what Amy had to offer. No, two cribs weren't necessary at the outset, but they'd be a good idea once the babies got more active. Definitely keep on with the breast feeding—things would be far easier on her if she did, even if the first two weeks would be difficult. All new parents were short on sleep and consequently short-tempered. . . . Give up on washing the babies' clothing separately in specialized detergent. Do everybody's clothes together in the baby soap, and it would simplify things tremendously. Unexpected and ultimately practical: Get a cordless phone that had both answering machine and speaker phone capabilities. That way, she could screen calls and talk with her hands free to get a chore done. The conversation went on, Amy mixing humor and encouragement and giving just the right amount of sympathy.

"Have you ever thought about going back to school and becoming a counselor?" Todd asked after the new mother hung up.

"Are you crazy?"

"Not at all. I just saw you in action, and you're terrific!"

"Right. As though I need any other demands on my time. School," she scoffed.

"You said you had taken some of the telecourses," he reminded.

"I was able to tape them and do the work at my convenience. Can we drop this?" Her face was a study of muted pain.

Sensitive to her distress but unaware of the cause, Todd decided to change the subject. "Can I ask you a few questions about when your sons were babies? I wondered a few things after I read the forms and the phone call triggered my memory."

"Hang on 'til I get the next load from the dryer." Amy snapped out of the past and pulled the next load out while Todd got them both glasses of lemonade. "All right. Fire away."

"Why did you bottle-feed the first set and breast-feed the second?"

Amy's hands stilled momentarily, then continued on with

her work. She didn't look up at him. "My husband wanted me to use bottles."

"That would make sense if he were helping feed them, but—"

"Was there anything else you wanted to ask?" she cut in.

Taking in her pink cheeks and avoidance of eye contact, Todd knew that he was treading on sensitive ground. He knew there were men who objected to their wives nursing their babies. The fact that Amy had chosen to nurse the second set and had done so for a prolonged period of time indicated that she was not in accord with her husband's wishes. *The guy must have been a real creep.* He decided he'd better move on to a different topic.

"What sleeping arrangements did you employ with the boys?"

"They shared a crib until they were about five months, then they each had their own. When the younger set was born, I just kept them in bed with me until they were four months, then put them in the cribs. The older set moved to a double bed with guard rails."

"Who helped you with the babies, and how much help did you get?"

"Friends from church helped out. I had two neighbors who helped with the first set. With the second set, a women's group I belonged to pitched in and helped until they were about five months old."

"A women's group?" he fished for further detail.

"Yes." She made it clear that she had said all that she planned to reveal.

"How much help, Amy?"

"Why are you asking me all of this?" Her eyes grew stormy.

"The first few years are extremely formative emotionally. If there were any constant caregivers other than yourself, I'd want to know about it," he explained evenly.

"There weren't." Her voice quavered. "My help was varied. I was the only constant. Are you satisfied?" Hostility shimmered under the surface of her very civil tone.

"I don't think the right person is getting the question, Amy. The question is, are *you* satisfied?" Todd sat in the living room and stared at the woman intently. Her hands froze midfold and hovered for a second. She gasped, then finished folding the shirt with jerky motions.

"You have no right—" she choked out.

"Perhaps I don't; but then, again, what damage is there in examining your life?"

"I will examine my own life if I choose to do so and when I choose to do so. I refuse to have some child psychologist waltz into my home, invade my privacy, and stick his nose in where it doesn't belong." Her voice shook with anger.

"My apologies, Amy. I didn't mean—"

"You did mean to, *Antares* Todd Avery. You plowed in where you knew you were unwelcome and rode roughshod over my pain. Let me put this to you plainly: I won't stand for your meddling again. If you so much as pry into any of my personal history again, I'll discontinue your study and report you to the university ethics committee." Gulping down a sob, Amy threw the shirt into the appropriate laundry basket and raced from the room.

"Mom! Hey Mom! Come see what I can do on the bars!"

Todd stood in the center of living room, stunned by Amy's outburst and wondering what to do. He turned and looked at the grubby little boy and stammered, "Your mom is kind of busy. Will I do?"

For the next thirty minutes, Todd sat out in the backyard and watched a full dozen children perform their latest tricks on the swing set and grass. He was a suitably impressed audience. The boys were consistent in confirming or denying his guesses at their identities. He was still right only half of the time.

Amy eventually made an appearance, looking somewhat subdued. She couldn't quite disguise the puffiness of her eyes or the telltale red nose that crying left in its wake. She had a big pitcher of the ever-present lemonade and cookies for all of the children. After they were done with their snack, she drew hopscotch and four-square on the patio for them to play. No matter what she did, she avoided looking at Todd.

"My mom said to give you this, Amy," Maise's daughter lisped. Her missing teeth made for some interesting sibilant sounds.

Amy opened the bag and smiled sweetly at the child. "Tell Maise thank you for me, darling. These are perfect." She pulled out several yards of ribbon and held them aloft. "Look guys—ribbons for the Olympics!"

"But they don't have writing on them," protested one freckle-faced boy.

"Mom puts the writing on with her special sewing machine, dork!" Mike jeered.

Zap. "Michael, that was unkind. Give an apology and sit in time-out for ten minutes."

"But Mom—"

"Do you want to make it fifteen for arguing with me?" Her jaw hardened.

Michael mumbled an acceptable apology as he slinked off to the time-out chair.

"I need some helpers to make the bean bags for the toss contest," Amy mused aloud.

"Me! Me!" came the raucous response.

Laughing, she selected two little girls and (zap) Dan and one other little boy. Four different colored socks were produced along with garbage bag ties and a big bag of pinto beans. Soon the children were measuring out the exact same amount of beans and filling their sock. It took a bit of cooperation, but they accomplished the task and sealed up the socks with ties.

"Okay. I'm a real rookie. Explain this to me," Todd said to Dan.

"Mom saves up all of the stray socks and lets us use them this way or to dust or make puppets. For the Olympics, we use them in the shot-put event."

"Not bad. Not bad at all," chuckled Todd.

❧

By supper, Amy had pounded out most of her anger on a meatloaf, and they ate in relative peace. The newspaper boy came to the door to collect, the phone rang twice, and a volleyball team captain came over to pick up the team's shirts. Amy sat back down and sighed as she looked at the meal. It was cold and unappetizing. She pushed her plate away and settled for a glass of skim milk and a few bites of salad.

Chores were done and the boys listened avidly to their story before they went to bed. "Mom?" Kenny asked drowsily as Amy bent over to kiss him good night.

"Yeah, Kenny?"

"Please don't fight with Todd and make him go away. Maise said you made Daddy go away because you always fighted."

"I don't want Todd to go away, either," Daniel asserted from the top bunk.

"Guys, I won't lie to you. Mom and Dad did fight. Daddy died before we could work our problems out. You guys fight with each other and still, when I give you a chance, you work things out. I just didn't have that chance. Now go to sleep."

"But don't make Todd go," Kenny insisted, holding her hand with a surprisingly desperate grasp.

"Todd is here for the summer, guys. After that, you know he has to move on." Amy gave each son a quick peck and left the room. The younger set were almost asleep already. She said their prayers with them and kissed them as they slipped off to slumber.

Once she was done, she stood in the hallway and pressed her spine to the wall. Her head fell back in defeat. *Lord, what are You trying to teach me? Why do I have to still ache from those terrible years? Please, Father, at least don't let my sons be tainted by the scars I bear!*

Steeling herself, she descended the stairs. She dreaded being alone with Todd.

Todd bowed over the scanner and stated in a neutral tone, "You were still in the high eighties with identifying the boys, Amy. I think I'm starting to see a few glimmers of a trend or two, but I'm not certain. I think after next week's Olympics, I'll be ready to see if you can't teach me the skills. For the next week, I want you to see if there is some reason why you identify the boys specifically."

His businesslike approach made it somehow easier for Amy to go on into the living room. She pulled over the last basket of laundry and absentmindedly folded the towels.

"Amy? Where are you? You're a million miles away." Todd stood in front of her, offering a glass of iced tea.

"Oh! Thanks." She reached over and took the glass, careful to not brush his fingers with her own. After taking a sip, she stated, "I was trying to count up how many ribbons to make."

"Why don't you call out the events, and I'll keep a running list? If they are pair or team sports, you need to tell me so I can allow for the extra ribbons."

Soon, they had a list of all of the events. Todd whistled

through his teeth. "This is a lot of work, lady. How do you do it all?"

"Really, the work doesn't take that long. I do all of the red and blue ribbons first because I can pre-set the machine to do the stitching in white. My only color change is for the white ribbons. I just put the name of the event and the year since the color of the ribbon speaks for itself."

"When I said you were one fine mother the other day, I wasn't flattering you, you know." His voice was sincere.

"Even if I am pretty messed up, myself?" she shot back bitterly. She heaved a sigh. "I'm sorry. That wasn't—"

"It was well deserved. You were right. I was way out of line today. I didn't mean to be. I've never had difficulty remaining objective about a study before, but the idea that you have had to do so much all by yourself just eats at me."

"I'm not complaining, Todd." Her voice was quiet and firm.

"No. No, you sure aren't. What is wrong with admitting that life isn't fair or easy, though?"

She gave him a guilty look. "I was just having a mini-pity party upstairs after I tucked in the boys."

"An incredibly short one."

She shrugged. "I'm not proud of myself when I have them at all. Complaints don't pay bills or bandage scraped knees. Self-pity doesn't make for happy children or cook the meals. I learned very quickly that if I was going to survive all of this, my attitude was either going to be my biggest ally or my worst enemy. When a mother doesn't have many choices, she does the best she can. I just count myself lucky to have a supportive church and good friends that bail me out if things get too hairy."

"How often does that happen? I've been around for five weeks, and I've never once noticed you needing anyone."

"Doc Garvey is Maise's boss. He takes the insurance

money as payment in full for all of the kids' care. Maise took the boys to and from school when I had the flu during the winter. Len Jackson across the street helps me with home repairs when I'm confronted with them. Some of the teens from the church baby-sit so I can go to Open House night and things like that." She threw up her hands. "I feel like I'm always having to lean on someone to get through."

"Since he gets four constant customers and refers troubled new parents to you for free counseling, I think Doc Garvey makes out pretty cheap. Maise's little girl is cute as a button, but you baby-sit for her fairly often. Same for the Jackson kids. You monogram for free for lots of those teens. The whole arrangement sounds well reciprocated," Todd logically pointed out.

"I guess that is what life is all about. Still, I appreciate them."

"Yeah, well, I think they appreciate you, too. There isn't any doubt in my mind that the boys are wild about you."

"I'm not so sure about that. . . ." Amy pulled a twisted face.

"Oh?"

"Ken and Dan are rather upset with me tonight."

"Did I miss something?"

"They are the ones who don't miss anything. They sensed the tension between us and are afraid I'm going to send you away." The confession was hard to spit out.

"Wow! They really are tuned in, aren't they?" Todd sat back and combed his fingers through his mustache thoughtfully. "So what did you tell them?"

"I told them that just as I give them time to work arguments out, we needed a chance to do the same. I also reiterated that you'd be leaving at the end of the summer. I think that is important for them to hear. They haven't ever had a man in their lives, and you've gotten far more involved with them than I had imagined. I'm afraid for them when you go."

"What have you done about the men you date? How have you handled things? We could use that as a good starting place."

"I don't date." Her voice was almost flat.

"Don't date? Come on, Amy. A pretty lady like you?"

"Get serious, Todd. No man in his right mind would be interested in a widow with four noisy, messy boys. Let's not delude ourselves."

"Then they're all fools. What is wrong with the boys? I think they're all great!"

"Yeah, well, there isn't any privacy whatsoever. It is always noisy, and they aren't exactly cheap to keep."

"Sounds more like a luxury convertible than a bunch of kids."

Amy laughed.

"I sure like it when you do that."

"What?"

"Laugh. I felt like scum, making you cry today."

"Can we just forget about that?" Amy asked thickly. Her mood shifted with amazing speed back to wariness.

"Whatever you want. I'm just sorry for hurting you, Amy. It wasn't my intent at all."

"Maybe not, but you can't delve into the past and bring me any happiness. I got off to a pretty rough start, and life has been real hard at times. I want to keep the past behind me and just make it through each day as it comes. Can't you just kick into your Gestalt Theory—you know, the 'here and now whole group' and let my past fade away?"

"Gestalt? Another telecourse?"

Amy nodded and shrugged. "Psychology and the Human Condition."

"I never bought into Gestalt. I think the past has a way of

catching up with us, often when we least expect or can least afford to cope with it. I guess I figure that the background is as important to the picture as the focal point."

"So that gives you license to act like Torquemada?"

"Torquemada? Is that how you think of me?"

"Not the monk part," Amy giggled nervously, but then suddenly changed to her somber self once again. "But yes, and someone who could have run the Inquisition to any painful conclusion. You're merciless."

"Ouch!" he winced.

"You did ask."

"I did. This is brutal to my self-image. I always thought of myself as an athletic Mr. Rogers."

Amy threw back her head and let out a howling laugh. When she finally wiped the tears from her face, she snickered, "Where is your cardigan?" and went off into hysterical giggles once more.

"Mommy? You aren't mad anymore?" a sleepy voice sounded from the stairs.

Amy didn't even turn around to look at the little boy. "No, Danny. Now go to bed."

As small bare feet padded up the steps, Todd looked at her with acute exasperation. "How did you know it was Dan?"

seven

The Olympics were a hit. Different parents came to help out each day. They brought snacks to keep the little athletes full. Lemonade was made in a big washtub, and folks helped themselves. Enthusiasm was never lacking on the part of the children or the adults. For the whole week, the five different colored, interlocking hula hoops hung from the patio, giving the youngsters their symbol.

Amy insisted that every participant got a prize for coming. She gave ribbons for first, second, and third places as well as bubble gum for anyone else that entered an event. Parents helped by counting somersaults, bar flips, and the like, so there would be several judges for accuracy. Polaroid pictures were taken for the kids when they received their ribbons. It was quite an event.

Todd loved watching the children put their hearts and souls into their efforts. He noted how Amy was just as likely to congratulate a loser as the winner, and often she consoled by pointing out that they had done better this year than last and that they were excellent sports. "We are here to have fun!" was her chant. The parents and kids alike echoed her words by the end of the week.

The last day of the event, she held a big barbecue and watermelon feast. All of the participating children and their parents came. The kitchen and picnic tables were piled with more hot dogs and ears of corn than Todd had seen since his meals in the college cafeteria. The sheer number of people dwarfed her huge backyard, yet Amy was completely unaffected.

"Aren't you going crazy with all of this?" Maise asked, trying to handle a plate and keep her daughter in sight. Todd leaned forward, wanting to catch Amy's answer.

"Not at all. We've lived through this twice already. It will take far more than this to do me in. As long as there's enough food, everyone will be happy. Pastor Jordan was nice enough to volunteer to man the barbecue, so I'm free to roam this year. That made things much easier!"

Even in the crowd, Amy kept tabs on the boys. At times, she had to ask Todd if he had seen one of them; but overall, they made out pretty well. Her accuracy rating for identification dropped to an all-time low of seventy-eight percent, though. Distracted as she was, her ability lost an edge.

The Saturday after the games were over, Todd slumped on the back steps and viewed the yard. "From the looks of things, a modern-day Sherman marched his army right through here on his way to the sea," he moaned. Paper cups, plates, streamers, and bits of latex from popped balloons littered the whole place.

"Then you should have seen it last year," Amy dissented. "Some joker brought a whole case of foam string that shoots out of a can. I thought I'd never get rid of all the mess!" She pulled down the hoops and stacked them neatly. "The kids will clean things up. Wait and see."

Much to his astonishment, several kids from the neighborhood appeared within the next hour. They pitched in and picked up the mess. "How did you—"

"Simple. They know I have a rule. . .pick up or don't come play again. They want to be in next year's games. One kid tried to skip out after the first year, so I didn't let him play the next as a reminder. I wouldn't have been so strict, but he was obnoxious and verbal about it. Now everybody takes me seriously. That's him, right there—the little blond guy in the striped tank top. He learned his lesson and was able to play again this year."

"Didn't he win something?"

"Yep. Second place for shooting the most hoops in five minutes. Nice kid. His parents just don't discipline him much. They were pretty upset with my ruling, but the rest of the neighborhood banded together and backed me up. So his folks decided if they couldn't make me back down, he'd better do his share of the work. Now he knows that he has to play by my rules at my house."

"You are something else, Amy Wilkins!" Todd merely shook his head.

After all of the excitement, the boys were ready for a quiet day. When all of the clean-up was complete, Amy sent her sons' playmates home with a treat and an invitation to participate in the next year's games. She then rattled her keys and called out to her sons, "Anyone up for a movie?" She was mobbed.

The Saturday afternoon matinee was full. They barely managed to find enough seats together. Loaded down with popcorn, Junior Mints, and cola, they settled into their seats and waited for the pre-feature cartoons to start. "Mom," a small hand tugged at Amy's sleeve.

"Hmm?"

"I gotta go!" came an urgent whisper.

Zap. "Oh, Mike! Didn't you take care of that before we left home?"

"I'll take him," Todd offered. "C'mon Mike. How about you other guys?" He hauled Mike and Ken out and returned a few minutes later with them in tow. In the darkened theater, it was hard to see, and they tumbled into empty seats just as the movie began. Amy was more than a little uncomfortable with the fact that Todd ended up sitting next to her.

For five and a half weeks, she'd carefully kept a distance

between them. The last thing she wanted was gossip about her and the doctor. She was smart enough to realize that with him in her home seven days a week, sixteen hours a day, there was ample opportunity for tongues to wag. Amy avoided any physical contact with him whatsoever—not even to share a hymnal or Bible at church. Nor would she allow him to open the van door for her. He'd gone along with her plan readily, as if he understood the motive behind her protective actions.

When a large hand slid over, Amy almost jumped. It simply took a fistful of popcorn and disappeared. She let out a soundless sigh of relief. After a few times, she didn't even pay attention to the action. The flick was an enchanting cartoon with several animals. Toward the end, John started coughing. "Here, honey. Sip the rest of my drink," Amy offered, handing the boy her cup. As she reached over Todd's lap, John's hand crashed into hers. The cup tipped, but she quickly righted the drink and shoved it into her son's hand.

Todd sucked in his breath. The ice-cold soda had splashed all over his leg.

"I'm so sorry!" Amy whispered. She grabbed the extra napkins from the empty popcorn tub and rapidly blotted at the fabric. "I can't believe I did that! I really got you," she empathized.

"Enough," he said quietly.

"Oh, Todd. You're still so wet!"

A large, warm hand slid down and stilled Amy's hand. Putting gentle, but definite pressure on her, he murmured in a husky voice, "Enough, Amy."

Something in his tone warned her she'd not been wise to make contact. She jerked away with a small cry. Luckily, the movie was at a place where several children were letting out small shrieks of alarm, so her noise went unnoticed. Her face burned with shame.

"We'll talk about this later," a deep voice declared in her ear.

Amy sat still and shivered.

For the rest of the afternoon and evening, Amy designed things to do that kept her overly occupied and in the midst of the boys. They made bird feeders with milk cartons and peanut butter dipped pinecones. They went on a rock-collecting walk down by the railroad tracks. For supper, they created homemade pizza. Any activity that would keep Todd at arm's distance and Amy surrounded by children was her mission. She attained her goal very admirably, at least until bedtime.

Once the boys were in bed, she suddenly recalled the need to sew. "I have to do some monogramming for the clinic jackets. Can you compile that data back home tonight?"

"I'd rather not. Why don't you settle down for a minute? You've been whirling like a tornado all day long."

"There's so much to do—"

"More like there is something, or someone, you want to avoid," Todd corrected her gently. He tugged at her hand and situated her in a chair. Her shudder wasn't lost on him. "Why are you so afraid of me, Amy Wilkins?"

She remained silent and shrugged. To deny the fact was useless. That much she knew.

Todd sat on the coffee table and leaned forward, resting his forearms on the part of his thighs just above the knee. "Are you afraid of gossip, or are you afraid we could have something pretty special if we ventured a try?" His voice was velvet soft and fraught with understanding.

"I don't want to have any relationships, Todd. I don't have the time or energy one deserves."

"That is a well thought-out line, Amy Louise. How often do you have to resort to using it?"

She sucked in a deep breath. Her eyes flew open, and she

stared at him like a frightened doe.

"I see I've ended up sneaking under your radar screen. No one else ever challenged that bit of motherly wisdom, huh? I'm not buying that line for a minute. After the boys are in bed, you could date. Any competent baby-sitter could feed them supper and tuck them into bed. They're well behaved and simple to entertain. You could easily be dating. They aren't toddlers anymore."

"Are you telling me how to run my life?" she shot back in a brittle voice.

Running a hand though his russet hair, Todd let out an exasperated sigh. "I don't know. I don't think so. Maybe a little. I only know that you are one fine woman, and I'm more attracted to you than any woman I've ever met. Five— almost six weeks together, and I've seen you in just about every state imaginable—upset, happy, exasperated, tired, cheerful, loving. There hasn't been any side of you, any facet of your personality that I haven't been able to take in stride. That's incredible, Amy.

"At the movies, I embarrassed you. I'm sorry about that, and I hope you know I am; but being by you in the dark and having your hand brush my leg threw us out of the ordinary and into a personal frame for the very first time. I think it took us both by surprise. I didn't mean to scare you. Certainly, I have no expectations of a sexual nature whatsoever. Such a move would be devastating to both you and the boys and highly unethical of me. Does that relieve you at all?"

"Okay." She still didn't meet his eyes.

"What I am going to say, though, is that when the study is over, things will be different. I am interested in you. Don't be surprised when I come to your door, pretty lady, because I don't plan on walking away from the sweetest woman and greatest kids any man ever stumbled across."

Her surprised gasp and stunned silence filled the room. The dryer buzzed. Taking the alarm as an excuse to get away, Amy leapt up. A warm hand encircled her wrist lightly and stayed her momentarily. "Saved by the bell?"

"Maybe," she choked back and then got away.

The next morning, Amy acted as if they hadn't had their discussion. In reality, Todd had rattled her badly. She had lain in bed, awake most of the night. All she could think about was her awful marriage with Joseph. He had started out so nice and kind. She was glad to get away from her father's drunken binges, so she got married the week she graduated from high school. Joseph's true colors appeared right away. A few weeks after the wedding, Amy had asked Joseph if she could go to college. He'd taken it as a personal insult, as if she'd implied he couldn't earn a living for them. He'd broken her arm that night. It was the first of countless violent episodes.

How long before she learned about Todd's other side? What was he like when he got mad? She shuddered at the thought. He was even bigger than Joseph, and she had the boys to think of. No, there wouldn't be any room in her heart for him. She would make sure of it. Then why had she cried, tears wetting her pillow for hours on end, in the dark of the night? Why did she suddenly feel so empty and lonely? It was awful.

&

They hurried through a pancake breakfast and got ready for church. Todd looked forward to Sundays, if only to see Amy prettied up. She wasn't a vain woman, but she did make an effort to look special on those days. She always wore a dress, even though pants were considered acceptable wear for the women. The fabrics were invariably soft and silky and whispered as she descended the stairs. Pantyhose made her shapely legs look sleeker, and the modest heels she wore gave more definition to the curve of her calves. Yes, Sundays were well worth looking forward to.

There had been a time when he'd looked forward to Sundays just to appreciate her appearance. Now, he anticipated them because the worship meant so much. She'd led him back to the altar to make a personal, spiritual commitment. Those moments had changed his heart and life completely. Out of the fullness of his heart, he'd come to see the Hand of God leading him. God had also fostered a love in his heart for Amy and the boys. Todd couldn't help wondering—could he lead her back to that altar now to make a different type of commitment?

Todd went to the Sunday school class with the younger twins that day. The older twins dallied, but finally turned up at their predetermined rallying point. According to their standard arrangement, they all met in the foyer after the worship service. Todd could tell that Amy had been crying. "Are you all right?" he asked softly.

"The service was a touching one," she murmured back, bowing her head.

"Really? I'll need to get a tape, then." Todd had been amazed that the church taped all of the services. Copies were available so that the elderly shut-ins, servicemen, and ill of the congregation could still worship. He stepped away, spoke with one of the sound technicians, and returned a few minutes later. "He already had a copy made." He patted his pocket and a smile of satisfaction creased his face.

"Oh." Amy mouthed. She drew her shoulders up and said, "We had better get a move on, team. If you are half as hungry as I am, the kitchen will be stripped bare in a half hour!"

They scrambled into the van and had soon happily devoured lunch. While Amy went upstairs to change, Todd grabbed the church bulletin and read the scripture references for the sermon. He was curious as to what had played on her emotions. The first passage caught his attention. . . . Psalm 147 spoke about praise, and then two verses stood out.

"He heals the brokenhearted and binds up their wounds. He determines the number of the stars and calls them each by name."

The follow-up scripture was Psalm 34:18: *"The Lord is close to the brokenhearted and saves those who are crushed in spirit."*

How did those apply to Amy? Just how deeply did her wounds go? Crushed in spirit? Brokenhearted? He wouldn't have ever applied either label to the young woman who bubbled all over this happy home. The part about the stars made a slow smile come to his lips. It was kind of neat, considering the terrible name he carried around. For certain, he would listen to the tape that night when he got home.

Once lunch was over, they went out to the backyard to play Frisbee. After awhile, Amy goy winded and sat out. Soon Todd and the boys were involved in a free-for-all tickle fight. "Don't break anything!" she called out. "Soccer practice starts tomorrow!" Her warning fell on deaf ears.

Later, Todd sat beside Amy on the porch swing. Each time she called a boy by name, he tried to determine what motivating factors made her decide which boy it truly was. At times, she was able to tell him why. Other times, some innate knowledge drove her. "Kenny hates the bars—to do that stunt, it had to be Dan." "John always takes a little skip before he jumps—Mike doesn't." "Oh, I don't know. That just sounds pure Daniel. No other kid in the universe would say such a thing!"

"Okay. Let's try something. Boys! Go behind the garage and switch shirts, or pretend that you did. I want to see if your mom can tell you apart." The boys complied with glee.

Moments later, they emerged. "Well?" Todd asked.

"Kenny is in the blue tank top. I'm not sure about the younger ones."

"Step four steps closer," Todd commanded.

The boys complied.

"John and Mike didn't exchange. John is still wearing green."

After confirming her identifications, Todd looked at Amy closely. "You knew the older ones from a distance, even before they spoke or you saw them in motion. It had to be something physical. The younger ones you had to see closer and moving. Possibly, their movements or their differences are less defined. What do you think?"

"I guess it makes sense."

"Try making a point of determining where your eyes go when you identify the guys—is it hairline? Mouth? Something in the facial expression or posture? Make note of these today and see if you come up with anything more specific. By Friday I'll be wearing jewelry, too. We fixed the original set to fit me comfortably, so I'm ready to go. I feel pretty dumb staying in the high fifties with as much contact as we've had with each other."

"I guess you can sympathize with their teachers, then. Even after a full school year, they can't tell the boys apart. Even worse, since the boys are only a grade apart, the teacher has the nerve-wracking problem for two consecutive years before she finally breaks free and clear of Wilkins twins!"

"There is a level of chagrin that goes along with this problem, Amy. To be unable to give a child his due because he has a look-alike is difficult for any professional. It feels like a terrible admission of incompetence."

"I'm not immune to that, Todd. That's why you're here. Even if we only determine what can be done for my four sons and no one else, I'll consider this a summer well spent."

"Would you?"

"I suppose I should feel contrite about that. I sound terribly selfish, don't I? *My* sons. I guess I'm parent enough to put their specific needs above all others. I'd love to see you stumble upon a greater truth so that every identical twin didn't have to be so infernally identical; but even if you straighten out these two sets, I'll be satisfied. I would consider that a real victory."

"You're right, it would be a victory. I don't consider your motives selfish at all. For a mother to put her children first is a rare phenomenon these days. More often than not, it is her job, or herself, alcohol, drugs, or her new husband or boyfriend. I know participating in the study is costing you far more than it's costing the boys. You don't get to sleep in or do laundry when you need to. You have had to be more modest than you might have otherwise been, cook for another hungry face, and wear that atrocious jewelry. I'm thankful, Amy. Truly, I am."

"Forget it, Todd. If you crack the mystery, the sacrifice is small potatoes."

"And if I don't?" he asked softly.

"Then I guess the boys got a good bit of sports coaching," she answered with a tipsy smile.

Late that evening, Todd made himself comfortable on his mother's couch and listened to the cassette tape of the church service. He wondered what the pastor could have said that went with those passages from the Bible. As the psychologist listened, he was impressed with the insight and wisdom that Pastor Jordan had into the human psyche. His sermon covered healing from emotional scars and moving from a crippled mental state to healing.

When the tape ended, Todd stood and stretched as he

thought about Amy. Her marriage was a disaster and her father an alcoholic. Her mother died when she was just fifteen. . . . Half aloud, he asked, "Amy Louise Wilkins, life has been really hard on you, even though you don't act like it. Did one terrible thing, one trauma hurt you, or was it everything all together?"

As he thought things over, Todd was baffled and saddened. He got ready for bed, but couldn't shake the deep regret he had about her secretive nature. Whatever it was, Amy was hurting terribly. She had tied his hands—he didn't dare confront her or question her or even offer her any insight or a shoulder to cry upon. To do so would be a direct invasion on her privacy, and she'd been crystal clear about that: Back off, keep out, off limits. The facade she maintained for her sons and everyone else about her must come at an incredible cost. How could he make her feel safe enough to be the *real* Amy around him—not just a community-minded citizen and picture-book mother? For all that he'd seen in his years of practice, he was sure nothing she'd endured would shock or disgust him. The only problem was, he couldn't reach out to her. At least, not now. Not until the study was over. After that. . .

☙

True to her word, Amy took the boys to soccer the very next day. Todd overheard her on the phone when she registered the boys for the team.

Her conversation had been interesting, to say the least. The registrar wanted to split the sets of twins apart—not by age, but by pair. "Separating them will be so much easier on the coach, and just think of the rivalry factor—certainly would juice up the games," she oozed.

"Frankly, I could do without that kind of rivalry in my home," Amy stated wryly.

"Oh, but—"

"And I'm sure you realize that as a single parent I cannot take my sons to their practice sessions if they're separated. The inconvenience you mention for the coach certainly can't compare to the inability I would have as a parent to see to my sons' safety and well-being."

"I suppose you have a point there," conceded the voice on the other end of the speakerphone.

"I do so appreciate your understanding." By the end of the conversation, all four boys were on the same team.

"Wow! Maybe you ought to go into phone marketing," Todd admired after Amy hung up.

Slumping against the counter, Amy rolled her eyes. "Never! I hate having to beg for favors like that!"

"Favors? Not quite. You have it all wrong, lady. They are providing service for a fee. You pay for the enrollment. Requesting the practical arrangement so the boys all get a chance to play and you can see to them is very reasonable. You didn't ask for them to get special numbers on their jerseys or insist on a special time for the practices. They were out of line, trying to make you jump through hoops."

"Do you really think so?"

"Let me give you an analogy. You go to the grocery store, and they tell you you can only buy things that have yellow on the label."

"That is ridiculous!"

"Yeah? Well, they were willing to take your money and then dictate what you could buy. You can bet they don't do that to other parents. Stand your ground, Amy. I'm proud of your assertiveness."

"If I was so great, why do I feel so wimpy?" she groaned.

"I'd better not answer that. Why don't you think about it though?"

"You mean to tell me Dr. A. Todd Avery is walking away

without offering advice?"

Replaying the tape from last night in his mind, Todd stood silent for a moment. After assessing her and giving her a long, hard look, he responded, "I don't presume to have all of the answers, Amy. More important, though—I won't discuss your feelings or personal matters unless you point blank ask me to because I refuse to make you uncomfortable or sad."

"Oh," she gulped.

"You've made it abundantly clear how dear your privacy is to you. I won't invade your domain. Not unless you invite me to do so. I don't want you to think I'm being glib, Amy. Far from it. I'm trying to be cautious."

"You don't want to endanger the study—" she began.

"Forget the study, Amy! I care about you. Somehow, some-where, you hurt. Until you decide I'm safe enough that you can open up to me, I'll keep to generalities and surface matters. Just know that I'm here, and I really do care. If you decide you can share any part of your pain, I'll listen."

"That's very professional of you, Dr. Avery."

"I wasn't talking as a professional, Amy. I was talking as a friend. Just as you find your sons get treated differently because of the identity crisis, know this: I understand it in a different way. I'm always judged and minced around for fear that I'll have some secret x-ray vision into the hearts and souls of ordinary people and uncover whatever it is they hide or fear the most. That isn't true. But I know full well that's how folks think. I go to parties or meet new people. Yet, they all clam up as soon as they learn that I am a psychologist. You don't expect a dentist to examine your teeth if you bump into him in the hardware store. Why do you think a psychol-ogist will treat you when you are leaning over the kitchen sink?" After his exasperated tirade, Todd let out a huffy sigh.

"I'm sorry—" Amy faltered. She wasn't sure she should

simply accept his blurted frustrations or run for cover. She glanced out to see the boys. All four were in the backyard, safe. Turning back around, she saw a hand raised right at the level of her face. She let out a small cry and flinched.

The glass in Todd's hand fell to the floor and shattered. "Amy?" he questioned hoarsely. His eyes roved her face intently.

Forcing herself to laugh, Amy pressed a hand to a heart that was beating far too fast. "I guess I'm on edge, after all. I didn't even hear you come over to the cabinet. Seeing that glass fall startled me."

"Oh." Todd seemed far from convinced. Looking down, he grimaced. "I'll clean up that mess. Let me get you out of here first."

"I'll get it—"

"Get serious, Amy. You're barefoot!"

"I'll just slip on my tennis shoes—"

"I'll have things cleaned up before then. We can't have glass on the floor like this. What if one of the boys comes in to get a drink or something?" he pointed out logically. "Now put your arms around my neck." He stepped a little closer, and Amy leaned back into the counter.

"Just go get my shoes. I'll stay here and make sure the boys don't get into it."

"If the Olympics were still on, I'd give you first place for stubborn willfulness. Now put your arms around my neck." Todd grabbed her wrists and wrapped them around his neck.

"You can't pick me up—I'm too heavy!" Amy felt the wild heat of a blush as Todd lifted her and made his way through the glass shards to the sewing room just off to the side of the living room.

"Where did you get a foolish notion like that?"

"I—well. . ." She shook her head. "Please—"

"Amy, I picked you up and tossed you in the pool and then carried you upstairs that same night. What makes you think I can't lift you? You aren't heavy at all!"

She made an inelegant snort.

"Most of the time, you eat the same amount as the boys. We go to a burger place, and you order a salad. At the church picnic, you ate like a rabbit and then ate that horrible pudding. How could you possibly be too heavy?"

"It all adds up," she mumbled in acute embarrassment to his chest.

"I agree. It all adds up to a very appealing shape. Soft, feminine curves that could drive any man to distraction. Now I'm going to put you down on the couch and let you read a magazine or relax for a few minutes while I go take care of the broken glass."

Amy let out a little gasp and squirmed to get free.

Squeezing her lightly, Todd chuckled. He set her down and slowly took his hands away. "You really need to relax, Amy."

She scooted away.

"Come on, Amy! It doesn't hurt to acknowledge that you are a fine-looking woman and real easy on the eye." He shot her a lopsided smile. "Besides, I really admire that ex-pensive jewelry you wear!" Without another word, he turned and sauntered back to the kitchen.

As soon as she heard the broom whisking across the linoleum, Amy scampered up the stairs. She changed out of her shorts and into a baggy pair of jeans. Was her floral-print T-shirt too tight? Troubled eyes scanned the mirror. No. To change shirts would be too obvious. Amy slipped on socks and tennis shoes and went back down. Crossing the kitchen, she ignored Todd's sweeping glance and called out through the screen door, "Come on in guys, almost time for soccer!"

Amy signed the boys onto the team roster and collected

the appropriate-sized uniforms. The boys already owned shin guards, but other than that, she picked up everything else—shorts, jerseys, socks, a jacket, all in dark and light blue. "I should have brought a bag or a laundry basket for all of their paraphernalia!"

"Why don't I take all this back to the van? There isn't any reason for you to have to stand here with your arms full," Todd offered.

"Are you sure?"

"No big deal, to borrow one of Daniel and Kenneth's favorite sayings," Todd declared.

Laughter gurgled out of Amy's rosy lips. "Maybe you *are* ready to tell them apart. You certainly can predict what they would say!"

The next two afternoons were spent in practice. The Wilkins boys comprised a full third of the team. Their monogrammed jackets and jerseys on the second day created a minor sensation. So did the dark blue on light blue team banner Amy made. Ken and Dan were the oldest boys on the team. Amy informed Todd with a relieved look, "They just made this team. Two months older, and they would be in a different division."

"I'm glad things worked out well." He popped the top on a can of soda and raised his brows and the can simultaneously, offering it to Amy.

"Thanks. They're going to start kicking drills. Is your jewelry on?"

Popping open a can for himself, Todd grimaced and nodded. "The fact that they're all dressed the same is going to make this a real chore. At a distance, they all look alike. The height difference is indistinct. Dark curls, same facial features. I figure I'll be doing well to hit twenty-five percent."

"Oh, how the proud are humbled," Amy razzed.

"Don't rub it in," he growled good-naturedly.

After downing a good swig, Amy smiled at him. "Get them thirty percent right, and I'll buy Chinese for dinner."

"Chinese?"

"Don't you like Chinese food?"

"I love it! I can't remember the last time I had it, though."

"Thirty percent, and you could be stuffing your face with fried rice, lemon chicken, sweet and sour pork—"

"Mu goo gai pan, egg rolls—"

"Straining chow mein through your mustache. . ." Amy twittered helplessly at the face he made at her assertion.

"You owe me paper-wrapped chicken or shrimp for that one, *Amy Louise.*"

"Not if you don't get busy and hit thirty percent, hotshot. Now who is that?" She pointed toward the water cups.

"Jonathan." He activated his fourth finger and waved toward the boy.

"Wrong. Michael." Amy zapped the child as well. She shot a smug look at Todd. "Hope you aren't too hungry."

"If I said what I was thinking right now, would you make me go to time-out, or would you have me make one hundred spitballs?"

"For what you probably have ricocheting between those ears, it would be time-out *and* your mouth washed out with soap!"

"Thirty point two percent," Todd declared proudly as they all sat back in the kitchen and he scanned the armbands. "Good thing I have a hearty appetite!"

"You barely squeaked by, and you know it. Okay team, hit the shower, then I'll take you out to Loys."

≈

By Friday, the boys were getting into the swing of soccer camp and looking forward to the matches that were dutifully penciled in on the calendar. Amy and Todd sat on the sideline, discussing which son was which. It was the middle of summer and sizzling hot. Amy began toting a big beach umbrella to the soccer field so they would have shade.

Amy fanned herself with a folded sheet of paper. "Whew! It's hot out here!"

Todd's face darkened. "It's over one hundred two, Amy. You can't keep wearing long pants out here. I've noticed you stopped wearing shorts, and I think you're crazy."

She peered over the edge of her makeshift fan like an old southern belle and teased, "Why, is that a professional diagnosis, Dr. Avery?"

Her attempt to divert him didn't work. He continued to scowl and growled, "You have to be roasting. No one in their right mind would come out dressed in such heavy clothing."

"Coming from a man who appeared on my doorstep in a jacket and tie, that's rich."

"Yeah, well, you'll recall I took them both off."

"Certainly you aren't suggesting I do the same." She arched a winged brow in a rather supercilious way.

"Before I rededicated my life to Christ, I would have answered in a heartbeat. Suffice to say, cooler clothing is called for. Wear your shorts, will you?"

"It seems to me you are the one who is hot under the collar, Dr. Avery," Amy taunted.

"Amy! Don't be so impossible."

"Perhaps you should examine why you are so controlling," Amy suggested neatly.

"If I were truly controlling, I'd have the boys steal every last pair of long pants you own so you'd be forced to put on a pair of shorts." Glowering at Amy, Todd shook his head. "You sure have a contrary streak in your nature, lady."

"I do as I see fit."

"Then stop having a fit and see if you can't fit back into shorts."

They didn't often disagree, but neither was willing to yield. Tension crackled between them for the rest of the afternoon. A message awaited Todd on Amy's answer phone when they got home. His mother was flying back in and would be at the airport at ten thirty the next morning. Her traveling companion had taken ill and needed to return home.

"I'll be over as soon as I get her settled back home," Todd declared.

Anxious to have some breathing space, Amy suggested, "Don't you think she'd like to visit with you for the day?"

"We'll chat on the way home from the airport, then she'll probably decide that there isn't any food in the fridge, hit the grocery store, go to another place to drop off all of her film, and still run errands after that."

"Are you kidding? Won't she be tired?"

"You don't know my mom very well."

"I've met her only once," Amy granted.

"She's absolutely terrified of flying. She uses special traveler's skin patches that make her drowsy, so she sleeps for the entire flight. My guess is that she'll be better rested than either of us."

"Still, you should take her on her errands—"

"Nothing doing. I have a job to do, and you can expect to see me here right around noon. Believe me, anything is preferable to standing next to my mom as she compares labels on the frozen peas and spinach."

"I've been known to do the same thing!"

❧

The house seemed strangely out of balance when the morning got underway the following day. Amy hadn't realized how much one person could fill up a room. The boys obviously missed Todd, too. They were real pests, all of them spending time sitting in time-out for a variety of infractions. In an effort to divert the boys to an activity, Amy gave them all squirt guns. "Now go and play in the backyard, will you please?"

Amy got some of her personal laundry done and carried it back upstairs. This was a good time to catch up on a few small things that seemed to keep slipping by. After picking up the bedrooms and putting fresh linens on the beds, Amy stuck her head out of the window and watched the boys cavorting in the backyard. "It's just about lunchtime. Why don't you come in and make yourselves peanut butter and jelly sandwiches?"

A lot of noise later, the boys called her to come downstairs. "We made a sandwich for you, too, Mom," Mike sang out. As she descended the stairs, all four of the boys pulled out their squirt guns and let loose a barrage of water.

"Not in the house!" Amy shrieked as she got thoroughly drenched. At that moment, her foot hit a small puddle and slid out from beneath her. An unchecked scream accompanied her fall, and she banged her head loudly as she tumbled the rest of the way down the stairs.

eight

"Mommy!" A hand rattled her shoulder.

"Are you—"

"—Okay?"

"Did she die?"

Fighting off the haze of pain and the beckoning darkness, Amy groaned. Her eyes flickered open and she choked down a wave of nausea.

"Mom, are you hurt?" Ken stuck his face right in front of her and demanded an answer.

Think. She had to clear her mind and think. "My head," she moaned, bringing up a shaky hand to rub the base of her skull.

"We're sorry, Mommy. Really—"

"Shhh, Johnny. Mommy needs to think," she faltered.

"Want me to call 9-1-1?" Dan offered solemnly.

"No. I'll lie down. I'll be all right." If only she could convince herself with those words. It felt much like all of those times after Joseph had knocked her around—fuzzy and indistinct, the agony of her body blunted by the haze of near oblivion. *Oh Lord, please help me. What would become of my boys if something happened to me? Jesus, I beg of you. . . .*

"Your foot, Mom," Mike said. "It's getting all big!"

His words broke into her desperate prayer. They also made her aware of pain in places she'd not yet cataloged. "I can feel it. You two little men go get me a bag of ice to put on it."

"Okay!" They pledged in unison, scrambling toward the kitchen.

"Dan and Ken, help Mom get to the sewing room. I'll lay down in there for a while." She strove to come up with a game plan. The boys helped her sit upright, and the room spun crazily. After taking a few deep breaths to steady herself, Amy tried to stand. Putting weight on her right foot was a mistake. Her body crumbled forward as she let out a yelp. In the end, she crawled to the living room and pulled herself onto the couch.

"Dan, put. . .a pillow under. . .my legs. . .Mike put the . . .ice bag on. . .my ankle. Be careful, honey—it hurts bad." Amy spoke through gritted teeth. Tears washed down her face, and she was helpless to stop them. Once she was situated, she urged the boys, "Go eat. . .Mommy needs. . .to nap." She raised her right forearm and covered her eyes, blocking out the kaleidoscope of worried faces and shimmering lights, and drying her eyes as well. She didn't want the boys to see her crying.

Oh, Father in heaven, how can this be? Please, take away the pain. Don't let anything major be wrong with me!

Shuffling steps sounded on the floor. A minute later, Ken touched Amy's shoulder lightly. "We decided to take turns sitting next to you. Dan wants to know if he should call Maise to come get Johnny and Mike."

"No," Amy gulped. "Maise is at work."

"What should we do, Mom? You're hurt bad. Your ankle—"

"What time is it?"

"Ummmm. Eleven-thirty."

"Todd will be here pretty soon, Ken. We'll be okay." Thirty minutes to hang on. Amy wasn't sure she'd be able to stay alert that long. Her head pounded unmercifully, and her blurry vision was not merely a result of her tears, either. She could hear Dan and Ken whispering, but couldn't concentrate well enough to comprehend what they said.

All the way back from the airport, Todd and his mother visited. Ruth was full of bits and pieces about her trip and amused him with the wild adventures she'd been on. "You sure haven't settled down with age," he teased.

"I'm just getting wound up. Now if I could just talk my son into giving me a grandchild. . . ."

Shooting her a sidelong glance, Todd said quietly, "If things go the way I want them to, you'll have four by Christmas."

Ruth was delighted and pumped him for all sorts of details. Todd was surprised to hear himself. He knew that he loved Amy and the boys. However, he hadn't admitted the fact aloud to himself, let alone anyone else. He warned his mother, "Amy is very guarded and skittish. She doesn't realize how strongly I feel about her, and I don't want to rush things right now."

"If she's half the woman you think she is, she'll come around." Ruth patted his hand. "So when do I get to meet them all?"

Todd glanced down the freeway to see the turnoff to Amy's street. "How about right now?" he asked impetuously. As soon as he drove up to Amy's yard, Todd knew something was wrong. Mike and John were in the front yard, unsupervised. Both ran up to the car before it stopped, hollering his name. "Hey, little men—what's up?"

"Mommy is hurt!"

"Bad hurt!"

Todd took in the news and the stricken little faces at the same time. He dashed up to the house and took the steps in a single bound. "Amy!"

"Here." Dan grabbed his hand and tugged him into the living room.

"Amy, honey." He gently pried her arm away from her face

and sucked in his breath. She was a ghastly shade of white, and tears streaked her face. He brushed curls away from the runnels of tears at her temples. "What happened? Where are you hurt?"

"Fell. . .stairs," she whimpered pitifully.

"Her foot is really big, and she hit her head," one of the kids offered.

"Why don't you boys go to the backyard for a moment?" Ruth had let herself in and had taken control. Todd shot her a look of relieved gratitude. "I'll help Todd see how your mother is. Then I'll come tell you how she's doing."

His strong fingers lovingly threaded through the dark brown curls and detected a large knot at the back of Amy's head. Air whistled through her teeth at the sickening sensation of even that tender pressure. Amy's eyes welled up again.

"Oh, honey, you really did it this time," Todd commiserated. "Let me see your foot." He scooted down toward the other end of the couch and carefully lifted the bag of ice the boys had provided. Her foot was already the size of a football. "Amy," Todd came back, hovering in front of her, "I'm going to check the rest of you out. Where else do you hurt? Can you move everything?"

"Got to couch. . . Can move everything," she gritted.

He lightly ran his hands over her, painstakingly thorough and slow. Her jaw was fine. As Todd traced her collarbones with his thumbs, he found them to be whole. He carefully checked her arms and ribs. The flare of her hips and the entire length of her left leg were exactly as they should be. "Amy, I need to turn you onto your side so my mom can see your back," Todd whispered in a choked tone. "It'll hurt while I turn you, honey."

Palms, slightly moist from nervousness, cupped Amy's face. Her eyes flickered open. They were cloudy and dull.

"Do it," she trembled.

A helpless cry escaped as Todd slid Amy to her side. "Shh, honey. I'm so sorry," he murmured. Her shirt had pulled out of her shorts a long while ago. He lifted it and nearly croaked at the sight of her back. The whole length of her spine was scraped and bruised. He cautiously felt her ribs for fractures, but found nothing. He looked away as his mother reached over.

"Her tailbone is worse than her spine," Ruth worried. "I got her insurance card and some ID from her wallet. Put them in your pocket and take her on in to the hospital. I'll stay with the boys."

Todd rolled Amy back and assessed her injuries one last time. "Amy, my mom is staying with the boys. We need to get you to the hospital. I can call an ambulance—"

"No."

"Okay, Amy. I'll take you."

"Boys."

"They'll be fine, Amy." Ruth smoothed Amy's wrinkled brow. "I'd love to get to know them, and I'll take good care of them for you. Did you want to tell them good-bye?"

Amy tried to nod and the movement wrenched a groan from her.

Todd spoke in a quiet tone that carried amazingly well, "Boys, come kiss Mom. I'm going to take her to see the doctor." All four tumbled into the living room, then froze. "Just give her a kiss, guys. She needs to get going," he prompted. After four slobbery pecks, Todd sent the boys out to the backyard.

Amy fainted as Todd picked her up off of the couch, and she didn't revive until he plucked her out of the van and carried her into the emergency room. His arms cradled her with infinite care, and he murmured tender reassurances to help keep the pain from overwhelming her. Amy's head sagged against his chest, and she bit her lip to silence her whimpers. The cool blast of the air conditioning hit them as the automatic doors opened.

"She fell down the stairs," Todd informed the triage nurse. She immediately led him from the waiting room to one of several cubicles. "She has a goose egg on the back of her head, and her right foot is huge. Her spine is scraped up something awful." Todd brushed his lips across Amy's temple, then gently laid her on her left side. As his arms pulled away, a desolate cry bubbled out.

"Oh, Amy. Not again," the emergency room doctor sighed as he stepped in. He shot Todd a venomous look and ordered, "Out!"

After giving a secretary Amy's insurance card and any of the pertinent data that he knew, Todd sat down. A few moments later, a social worker approached him and asked him to accompany her. Seated in a small, sterile room and provided with a cup of scorched coffee, Todd wondered what was up. "How is Amy?"

"They have her down in radiology right now. They need to do x-rays of the foot and ankle as well as the skull. Dr. Avery? It is doctor, is it not?"

"Yes. My doctorate is in the field of psychology," he clarified.

"Can you tell me what happened?"

"I don't really know for certain. Amy said she fell down the stairs."

"You don't know?"

"I was picking my mom up from the airport, and we swung by so that she could meet. . . Hey! What is this all about?" As concerned as he had been, Todd hadn't allowed the ramifications of this meeting to register.

"The emergency room doctor asked me to discuss the

cause of Mrs. Wilkins's injury with you."

"Did he?"

"Yes. Where was she when you entered the house?"

"Amy was on the couch in the living room. Listen—you can simplify this whole matter. Call her home. My mother is there and can vouch for my whereabouts. Her sons can tell you precisely what happened. I resent this whole setup."

"Certainly, given Mrs. Wilkins's current condition and her history, you must see that the doctor reacted appropriately."

"Her history?" Todd leaned forward. "Just what do you mean by that?"

Pursing her lips together tightly, the social worker stood. "I'll call Mrs. Wilkins's home now, Dr. Avery. Thank you for your cooperation."

"Now wait a minute. I think I deserve an explanation, if not an apology."

"I'm afraid more than enough has been said. Would you care to remain here or in the waiting room?"

"I'd rather stay with Amy."

"I'm sorry, Dr. Avery. Our policy is absolute: Any woman with unexplained injuries is to be kept from the man bringing her in. Until I can corroborate your version, we cannot allow you access to Mrs. Wilkins."

Biting back the urge to let out a loud roar, Todd pasted on his I'm-in-control look and nodded tersely. "I'll be in the waiting room. As soon as you 'corroborate my version' I insist that I be taken to her immediately."

"We'll see about that." The social worker gave him a chilly nod and minced out on heels that were far too high.

"Dr. Avery?" A long while later, a soft voice sounded from behind him as a hand rested on his shoulder. "Amy is back from x-ray. Her sons and your mother vouched for your innocence." The nurse's face was empathetic. "You know, I'm sorry they put you through all of this; but with what we see come through here, we try our hardest to protect these women."

"Disgruntled as I am, I do appreciate that," he allowed. "How is she?"

"Why don't you come on back? Doc will be in with her in a minute."

Todd was directed back to the small cubicle and stood there quietly. Amy's chart rested on the counter. He fought with himself mightily. Did he dare open it and peek? No. He knew he shouldn't. As badly as he wanted—*needed*—to know, he couldn't bring himself to snoop. "Amy?" He bowed over her and brushed his knuckles over her cheek.

"Hurts," she whispered hoarsely.

"I can believe that. You did a real bang-up job."

"Side."

"You want to be on your side, honey?"

"Please." Her voice was a vague croak. With all of the tenderness he could muster, Todd slipped his hands onto her and coaxed her onto her side. She bit her lip and still moaned.

"I'm sorry, Amy. Let me—"

The curtain was pulled back and the physician stepped in. "Amy, you broke clear through the ankle. A couple of the bones in the foot also got crunched. Swollen as it is, I can't cast it. We'll splint it for now and keep it iced. Day after tomorrow is the soonest I'll be able to put a cast on it."

"What about her head?" Todd inquired.

"She undoubtedly has a concussion. I'll keep her until tomorrow so she can be observed. The catch here is that since we need to stay on top of her neurological functioning, she can't be given pain medication. Narcotics can alter mental functioning and mask important symptoms."

"Nothing?" Todd pursued, disbelieving his ears. "She's in a lot of—"

"I know." The doctor cut him off. "Amy and I go way back. I know she's tiny, but she's a tough lady, aren't you, Amy?" A heavy hand rested on her shoulder, and she nodded almost imperceptibly as if on cue. "You're welcome to stay with her. We'll splint her now and then take her upstairs."

Todd stayed with Amy while they tended to her ankle and helped push her gurney upstairs. At suppertime, he coaxed her into taking a few meager bites of the gelatin and soup. Pain ravaged her face, and she struggled to keep from moaning each time she exhaled. Todd tenderly traced his fingers over her lips. "Let go, Amy. You don't have to be brave." He continued to speak to her gently, using his voice to anchor her to the reality of his caring presence.

Amy couldn't bear to use the bedpan, so he carried her back and forth to the bathroom, diplomatically leaving her to the nurse's care in the interim. Though her cheeks bore an embarrassed flush, she whispered her thanks. He combed her hair, doing just the sides and front and leaving the back alone for fear that he might accidentally touch upon her lump. Most of the time, he sat and stroked her arm gently, quietly encouraging her to rest. He tried to be soothing and comforting. She felt hideous, but he did his best to take the sharpest edge off of the pain. At eight-fifteen, he called her home and let each of the boys tell her good night. Ruth gushed on and on about how wonderfully behaved the boys had been.

"You must be tired. Go," Amy urged him.

"Unh-unh. Not a chance, pretty lady. I'm staying right here." Once again Todd sat down in the chair he had pulled next to the bedside and threaded his fingers with hers. "Why don't you see if you can drift off, honey? I know you have to be tired, and while you sleep, you won't hurt so much."

"Can't sleep."

"Okay. Just close your eyes and rest." He tenderly rubbed his hand down her arm. She recoiled from his touch. "Amy," his chide was gentle.

She whimpered. Unsure why she was rejecting his touch, Todd settled for enveloping her hand in his.

The nurse came in and checked on her. "When can she have something for the pain?" Todd drilled.

Shaking her head apologetically, the nurse explained, "Not 'til morning. Narcotics affect dilation of the pupils and cloud mental functioning. If she starts having problems related to the concussion, I won't be able to see it because of the drugs."

Turning his back to Amy, he murmured in a low tone, "What about hypnosis?"

The nurse's eyes widened. "Nothing wrong with it, I suppose, but no one here can do it." Getting a look at his sardonic grin, she raised a brow and smiled as he nodded.

Todd perched on the edge of the bed and drew circles on the back of Amy's hand with his thumb. "Amy, I can help you go to sleep. I need your permission, though."

She made a small, indeterminate sound.

"I want to hypnotize you. They can't give you any drugs, and it's plain you need comfort."

A voice from the doorway said, "It's a good idea, Amy." Pastor Jordan came in and stood at the other side of the bed. "Why don't we have a word of prayer, then Todd can use his talents? He's an ethical man who's made a generous offer to help."

"I don't want to be out of control," she confessed.

"Amy, none of us are in control. When we give our hearts to Christ, He is in control," Pastor Jordan reminded her. "Frequently, that means He leads us on paths we wouldn't have chosen. Todd is a brother in Christ. He's trying to minister to you. Let him. Otherwise, you may be binding the very hands God sent to care for you."

The pastor prayed for her, then slipped out.

Todd asked, "Are you ready?"

Amy wearily opened her eyes just a slit. She swallowed hard, as if the decision were almost too much for her, then she whispered, "Okay."

"I won't make you sorry, Amy." He took her hands in his and slowly rubbed them with his thumbs. "Close those pretty, deep blue eyes and float away. There you go." He kept a steady stream of words going in a lulling monotone. He knew she had no notion what he wanted of her, but he kept his tone so velvety, so coaxing, that she complied. Slowly, her tension and pain drained away. He continued to speak softly, tenderly, until he could tell that she was finally asleep.

Todd gently straightened the covers over her, then whispered, "Lord, please comfort her."

The nurses switched shifts at eleven o'clock. He could hear them exchanging information outside the doors of the patients' rooms. Amy's nurse had sent Todd down to the cafeteria to get a quick bite and didn't realize that he had returned.

Outside the door, he could hear the nurse's muted voice. "Mrs. Amy Wilkins. Twenty-seven-year-old female. Fell down a flight of stairs. Moderate occipital concussion with neuro checks every two hours. So far they are within normal limits. Skin integrity along entire spine length impaired. Fractured right tibia at ankle level. Three metatarsals cracked. She's splinted. No pain meds, and she could certainly use them. She's a widow, but a friend of the family stayed to help—he's down at the cafeteria right now. He's good with her. Carries her to the bathroom, got her to sleep. He's a psychologist of some type. Hypnotized her. The cause of her injuries is confirmed, but she had a past history of two years worth of severe domestic violence that she wants kept confidential. Be careful with her medical records. Chart is kept at desk instead of the door pocket. Any questions?"

Todd was stunned. The emergency room staff had alluded to it, but he'd been so focused on caring for Amy, nothing registered yet. He slipped into the bathroom quietly while the two nurses chatted a moment more before entering the room and checking on Amy. After they left and proceeded down the hall to the next room, Todd resumed his seat next to her bed and tenderly trailed his fingers down her pale cheek.

All of the pieces to the puzzle finally fit. No wonder she didn't keep pictures of her husband around or speak of him. Of course she didn't date. The day they had the argument and he broke the glass, she must have thought he was going to strike her! That day in the pool, she was crying—not because she hit her head, but because he had scared her; and she had cringed when he wanted to find the bump then, too! She got "way crazy" when the boys reverted to physical violence. The way she had identified with the sermon about being shattered in spirit and heartbroken. All such seemingly small, insignificant things. Apart, they meant nothing. Within the proper framework, they spoke volumes. Tracing her cheekbone, Todd sighed, "Oh, Amy. . . ."

The next day, he carried her into the house and laid her on the bed in the sewing room. The boys gathered flowers and put them in a peanut butter jar to perk up the room. They were subdued. Satisfied she was not going to suffer ill effects from painkillers after an overnight observation, the doctor had ordered medication for Amy. Todd filled the prescription at the hospital so they would have the medication with them right away.

"Where's my jewelry?" Amy murmured as Todd gently laid her down.

"Don't worry about that now."

"Yes. Want it on. See if I do better or worse like this," she persisted.

"Amy, I'm going to keep the boys outside, and I'll be zapping them, myself. You don't need to—"

"Yes. Please." Her eyes were almost glassy from the narcotic she had been given before being discharged, and her voice was slightly slurred.

"Son, give in. It won't hurt anything, will it?" Ruth directed the words to Todd but stood at the bedside smiling winsomely at Amy. "Dear, you have marvelous children."

"Thank you for watching. . . ," Amy mumbled.

"Shhhh." A slender, tapered finger pressed against her lips. "I loved being with them. For the next little while you'll need a lot of help. You just tell Todd to let me know what you want. Now I'll help you slip into a nightie, then I want you to fall asleep."

While Todd went to get the laser band, Ruth helped Amy change into a simple cotton duster. Todd tapped on the door, and Ruth admitted him. He knelt at the bedside and hesitated before finally putting the apparatus on the woman he had come to love. After he finished, he gently squeezed her hand. "Sweet dreams."

Todd walked his mother to the door and gave her the keys to his Corvette. Ruth laughed and said, "Todd, she is a dear, and the boys will make wonderful grandsons. I'd tell you not to make me wait too long, but I know you are already serious about this gal—otherwise you'd never let me drive your car!"

Amy couldn't hear the conversation. All she distinguished was a deep laugh mixed with a higher one, then the door closing. Moments later, the car hummed away. As mentally fuzzy as she was, she thought Todd had left. Throwing back the covers, she tried to sit up.

"Oh, no you don't."

"Todd?" Amy stared at him as though he were a figment of her overly active imagination. "You left—"

"You think I'd go and leave you like this? Oh, Amy, never!" He strode across the room and made her lay back down. "You have to keep your foot elevated, or we can't get a cast put on it tomorrow."

"I'll lay on the couch or on the lounger in the backyard," she offered, her voice strangely vague.

"Don't fight the sleep, Amy."

"My boys—"

"Are all fine. I have them picking lemons for lemonade, and I'll take them for a bike ride later on. Don't worry about them, Amy. I'll keep them safe and happy."

"Thank you. . ." Soft lips kissed her drooping eyelids closed and then butterflied across her temple. *I must be dreaming,* she thought as he murmured something she couldn't quite understand.

Throughout the day, Todd and the boys sneaked to the doorway and checked on Amy. Pain, exhaustion, and drugs combined to make her sleep long and deep. The boys rode bikes while Todd did yard work, then they ran through the sprinkler in the backyard. Ruth left a tuna noodle casserole for them, and Todd popped it into the oven, grateful for his mother's insight. Since Amy always made salad in a huge bowl, there was plenty left for supper. He went back out to be with the boys.

The house was strangely quiet when Amy awoke. She lay there, disoriented for a while, and finally gathered herself enough to make an effort to determine her sons' whereabouts. Eyeing the splint, she knew without a doubt that she couldn't walk on her foot. She could hop or perhaps crawl. When she sat up and let her feet dangle over the edge of the bed, the whole room swirled madly about. Hopping would never work. Desperate as she was, the humiliation factor didn't much matter; so she started to crawl, even though her effort was a poor one. Just as she reached the hallway, Todd's big feet came into view.

"Amy Louise Wilkins!" he howled. "What in the world are you doing?" He swooped down and swept her up into his arms. The action made her lose her equilibrium. She closed her eyes and clutched wildly at his shirt. Todd asked in a far softer tone, "Dizzy?"

She nodded pathetically.

His arms tightened around her, and his chin nudged her head closer still. "Take a deep breath. Good, honey. Now blow it out slowly. Okay, another one."

Amy followed his directions almost mindlessly. His instructions worked. Her head cleared. "I'm all right," she whispered.

"You could have fooled me. What are you doing out of bed?"

"The boys—"

"Call me next time, honey."

Amy gave no reply.

Squeezing her gently, Todd declared with hyperbolic humor, "Promise me you'll call me, or I'll stand here holding you 'til we're both old and gray."

"You wouldn't!"

"Wanna try me?"

Amy sniffed with dramatic disdain. "I know such an outrageous thing could never happen. You'd get too hungry standing here. I'd also break your back after about two minutes."

"Wrong, little lady. I've been standing here longer than two minutes, and I could hold you like this all day. Where did you get the cockeyed notion that you're heavy? You said much the same thing that day the glass broke in the kitchen. You baffle me completely."

"Sure," Amy scoffed.

"Have you ever known me to lie, Amy?"

"Nooooooooooo," she drew out the word thoughtfully. She then hastened to add, "But there's always a first time for everything. You've probably been on your best behavior, kind of like a honeymoon."

"Amy, if we were on a honeymoon, my behavior would be remarkably different. Most remarkably." He looked down at her with an expression that made her breath freeze. Her throat went dry, and she could feel the heat in her cheeks.

Todd let out a deep, throaty chortle. "I've made a grown woman with four sons blush! Amy, you're full of delightful surprises."

He carried her to the kitchen window so she could peek out at her sons. After she assured herself they were all fine, she caught her reflection in the windowpane. Amy gasped and lifted her hand to her hair. "I'm a fright!"

"You're beautiful. Would you like to wash up, though?"

"Please!"

He carried her into the lavatory. As he cupped her ribs to balance her, he said in a low, confidential tone, "Listen, Amy—you're not very steady. I'll leave you alone, but if you get dizzy. . ."

A small sound of embarrassed fright bubbled out of her.

Todd gently gathered her into his arms. Too embarrassed to face him, Amy let her forehead drop and rest against his chest. He drew her closer. It was a gentle, undemanding hug, quiet and supportive without any real passion. She stayed there for a while, her wits still scattered and nerves frayed.

"Okay, honey." Warm lips kissed her crown. "I'll give you a few minutes," he whispered.

Amy barely managed to contain herself until the door clicked shut. She melted onto the commode, grabbed a towel, buried her face in it, and started to sob.

nine

Amy was drifting again. Todd had given her two more pain pills after he gently washed her face and hands with a deliciously warm washcloth and carried her back to bed. Thankfully, he ignored the obvious fact that she had been crying.

"Mom?"

"Yeah, John."

"Don't forget to zap me," he reminded. He waited a few seconds for his mother to use the laser system. "I wondered if you wanted me to read a story to you tonight."

"Oh, pumpkin, you're so thoughtful." She opened her arms, and he willingly slid in to receive a hug. "I'm pretty tired."

"Maybe tomorrow, sport," Todd suggested from the doorway. "I'd like to have you go get your brothers. It's time to wash up and eat chow."

"If you say so." The little boy looked hesitant.

"John." Zap. "Your mother needs to rest right now."

Looking at her, John nodded. "Okay. You're right, too."

"Huh?" Todd looked at the boy in bafflement.

"I'm John," the child provided him with a wicked grin as he scurried on out the door.

Amy's weak chuckle and Todd's self-satisfied laughter mingled in the late afternoon peace of the home. After she caught her breath, Amy asked, "Todd, please bring me the phone."

"What do you need?"

"The phone."

"I understood that was what you wanted, but why? You're supposed to be sleeping."

"I need to call Maise. It's getting late."

"Late? Late for what?"

"The boys. . .tonight. I can get up tomorrow, but I don't think tonight—"

"Amy Louise, are you crazy?" Todd sat on the edge of the bed and stared down at her. "It's all been taken care of. Mom and Maise and Pastor Jordan got together on a conference call and worked out the details. Mom will watch the boys while you get your cast tomorrow. Maise will stop in and do laundry on Friday, and Pastor has two of the church women coming in tomorrow night and the next night with meals."

"Why? I—"

"Honey, let us help you out here. Lie back and rest. If you need anything, you just yell for me."

"*You?* But—"

"You can't very well be left alone and certainly can't be left all alone with four little boys!"

"But you can't stay!" She jolted into full consciousness.

"Of course I will. I'm the logical choice. Maise has to work, and I know the boys' schedule better than anyone else. This way, I can continue the research as well."

"But you're a *man!*" she burst out, her eyes wide with shock.

"True. I always have been," he agreed with maddening simplicity. He then added wickedly, "I was wondering if you'd noticed."

"No."

"You hadn't noticed?"

"Stop muddying the waters, Todd. No. You can't stay."

"There are only two reasons I can think of that would motivate you to object. First off, you're completely and utterly safe. Even if you weren't in dire physical straits, we both know that you aren't promiscuous and the boys make amazingly competent chaperones. I think that puts that issue to rest.

Secondly, if you're concerned about what everyone else might say, then grow up. Your family's welfare comes before malicious gossip. Pastor even knows I'm staying, and he didn't seem to balk about it at all. I don't think you'll get a better moral endorsement than that!"

"Oh." Amy sagged back into the mattress, feeling suddenly very spent. The quick spurt of energy was all that she had. The pain pills were strong.

"Yeah. 'Oh.' Now close your pretty blue eyes and coast. Do you feel like eating something now, or would you like me to nuke it later on?"

"Later, please," she mumbled. Her eyes seemed too heavy.

"Fine by me. Sweet dreams."

His hand cupped her cheek, and she let her head loll that direction on the pillow so his hand continued to hold her. It was such a good feeling, safe and cozy. Mumbling from the medication, Amy said as much. She also said more, but it was slurred with drugged sleepiness.

❧

When Amy was completely asleep, Todd reclaimed his hand. As he let go, he murmured his regrets. "You won't even remember saying those nice things to me, sweet Amy. Those walls you put up are so strong. Still, if you can't admit them to me when you're feeling like yourself, it's good to hear them when you're half gorked. At least I know how you really feel. With God's help and healing, I'll make you feel safe enough to say them again someday."

Down the hallway, four little boys were making a disaster area of the bathroom under the pretense of washing up for supper. Were it not for the fact that they might catch sight of the act, Todd would have bent low and kissed Amy. Good-naturedly grumbling under his breath, Todd muttered something to the effect of four pint-sized chaperones being unfair.

The boys ate and goofed off a bit more than usual at the supper table. Knowing children as he did, they behaved just as Todd anticipated. They'd been worried and subdued for a full day and night; merely having their mother back under the roof was reassuring. He permitted the high jinks to a certain level and then put a stop to them. "Remember that your mom is sleeping," he stated in a grave voice.

The boys cleared the table, did the dishes, and swept the floor as usual. They argued about whose turn it was to do each of the chores, but Todd stepped in and assigned them. He made use of the laser, zapping and calling out names like a Marine Corps sergeant. The boys were surprised when he called them correctly and amused when he didn't. Todd wondered how much capricious exchanging was occurring, but it was too much to sort out. He hadn't slept much last night in the sagging recliner at the hospital.

Baths were over and pajamas on. The boys congregated in the living room. Todd did nighttime devotions and looked at the boys in a whole new light. Someday soon, if he had his way, these boys would be his sons. As he tucked Dan and Ken into their bunk beds he asked, "Have you guys read any of the Hardy Boys mysteries?"

"Huh-uh. Are they good?"

"Real mysteries?"

"I used to have a whole set of them. I'll see if Grandma Ruth still has them lying around someplace. They're about these two boys and their friends. They solve all sorts of interesting cases."

"Know what?" Dan asked, propping himself up on one elbow.

"What?" Todd waited, cocking a brow.

"We don't have a grandma."

"Yeah, we do," Kenny refuted. "Dad's mom—but she lives far away, and she never bothers with us."

"Anyway," Dan sighed, "I really liked your mom. She's pretty cool. Do you think it's okay with mom if we really call her 'Grandma Ruth,' or do you think it will make her upset?"

"Why don't you ask her in the morning?" Todd fielded the query without a hitch. Boy, he may have blown it there. His mother had the boys call her that yesterday, and it somehow felt right. The only problem was, how did he explain it to Amy? He wandered down the hall and caught himself whispering one of Amy's lines, "Two down, two to go."

John and Mike were having a minor pillow fight. Todd broke it up by merely grabbing each and throwing them onto their bunks. "I'm supposed to be on the top!" protested one.

Zap. "I don't think so, Mike. You're the ground floor man in this pair. Nice try, though."

A bit of grumbling ensued, but both boys snuggled in. "Todd?"

"Yes, John?" Zap.

"Do you really have to go away at the end of the summer? You're lots of fun. I even like Grandma Ruth. Maybe you should both come live here with us."

Thinking quickly, Todd asked, "Do you seriously think this house could hold all of us?" He flicked off the light in the silence that followed. He turned to leave and was stopped dead in his tracks.

"Maybe not all of us unless two of the grown-ups sleep in the same bed in Mom's room. The sewing room bed is too little for two."

"Sounds like you've been giving this some thought," he countered. "For now, though, it is bedtime."

"Maybe we can work something out. Can we talk it over another time?"

"Perhaps," Todd evaded, leaving swiftly before any more was said. Kids sure had a way of uncovering issues.

In the past, Todd watched Amy after the children were in bed. It seemed as if she lived a whole extra lifetime in the hours between eight-thirty and morning. She'd sort laundry, do a load or two of it, mop floors, pick up a stray toy, unknot shoelaces, mend clothes, monogram, pay bills, clean the refrigerator, dust the furniture, or find some other small but necessary task to do. He had taken to helping her for a short while and then settled down to scan the ID bands and tally scores. Tonight, he tried to prioritize.

"What would you do, sweet Amy?" he mused aloud.

Amy was forever reminding the boys to put their socks in the hamper. Every time she did laundry, there were all sorts of stray socks. Todd understood why as he noted a sock peeping out from beneath the bunk bed and another on the floor by the dresser. There was a pair by the boys' upstairs bathroom sink, one in the hallway, and a few more scattered about. He finally rounded up seven of the silly things—and none of them matched! Shaking his head in amazement, Todd tossed them into the hamper.

He remembered the condition in which the boys had left the downstairs bathroom. It didn't take long to tidy up the disaster, but when Todd put the lid down on the commode, he let out a deep sigh.

Amy's knees trembled, and she'd made that panicky noise when he'd braced her by the sink. He couldn't help overhearing her weeping when he'd stepped out to give her privacy. Had her husband treated her badly in their intimate life, too? The thought rocked him.

He longed to heal her with his love and couldn't stay away. He walked down the hall to check on her. She still slept soundly. Todd watched her for a few moments, his eyes caressing the riot of curls that framed her face. Her lips were relaxed into a hint of a smile—a welcome change from last night. Seeing her hurt without anything to help her through the pain had bothered him greatly. Assured she was comfortable and not wanting to disturb her rest, Todd quietly left and scanned the armbands for data. Even heavily medicated, Amy was right seventy-eight percent of the time. Todd tried to think of what cued her into the boys' identity. . . her vision was slightly blurred and her eyelids heavy, so many of the tags were done based on what—sound? Intuition? Gross body movement or posture? He wasn't sure.

When he reviewed his own tagging, Todd's jaw dropped. His normal fifty-fifty accuracy had jumped to sixty-nine percent! *Why?*

A small sound from the sewing room brought him to his feet. Amy was restlessly adjusting to a new position. Her splint caught in the edge of the twisted lightweight blanket. Todd hovered over her and decided to untangle the whole mess. He'd barely drawn back the blanket when he realized Amy was half-awake. He lifted his hand to smooth back her hair.

ҙ

Eyes wide open with shock and panic, Amy flinched. Her hands flew up in a purely defensive move. She swiftly curled up into a ball and whimpered, "No, please no—" She stayed in that position, waiting for blows to rain down. Her muscles knotted, and her nerves stretched to the screaming point. It wasn't just a nightmare. He was really here. Big hands, hurtful hands, rested on her shoulders. She could feel Joseph's breath on her cheek. She scrunched her eyes shut, desperately wishing him gone and quailing under his restraint.

"Amy, it's Todd. You're safe, honey. It's Todd. Todd."

At first, her panic didn't let the words penetrate. By the time the words sank in, Todd had wrapped her in the sheet and lifted her into his arms. He sat on the edge of the bed, cradling her and rocking her as if she were a small, frightened child. The sensation of being cared for and protected was too much. A torrent of tears broke loose. Those magical arms enfolded her, and Amy spent her fright and grief, shuddering in revulsion as the memories surfaced and were drowned in her tears.

When her weeping finally tapered off, Amy slumped against him, her emotions and body spent. Should she try to regain the shreds of her pride, or could she avoid everything and fall into an exhausted sleep?

Softly kissing her hair, Todd murmured, "Never again, Amy. No one will ever hurt you again. That part of your life is all over. You can put it behind you."

"I'm sorry—"

"You're sorry? For what?"

"I–I—you can let go of me now."

"Maybe I could, but I don't particularly want to. I like holding you, little lady; and right about now, you could stand a friend."

"But—I—"

"You have nothing to be sorry for, nor ashamed of, Amy. The way Joseph treated you was his fault. His problem."

"You know." Her voice was thick and flat.

"Yes. You didn't have to keep such things a secret, Amy. If anything, you should be proud of yourself. You've lived through the worst of life and came out victorious." His voice was deep and steady, and his arms hugged her close.

The room was silent, and then Amy started to cry softly once again.

"Mommy?"

Todd cupped Amy's head to his chest. "Mom isn't feeling very good right now, Dan."

"I didn't think so."

"Go ahead and get yourself a drink of water before you go back to bed."

"Will you take care of Mom?"

"Of course I will."

"Okay." Footsteps padded up three stairs and then came back down. "You didn't zap me."

"I took off the jewelry," Todd sighed.

"Then you can write in the nighttime book that you were right. I'm Dan." They heard feet pad up the stairs, water run, and the small, distinct thump of a seven-and-a-half-year-old boy falling into bed.

"I knew."

Amy asked quietly, "Is it that noticeable? That obvious?"

"Huh? Oh! I meant that I knew that it was Daniel, and I didn't even see him. This is kind of spooky."

A small, tense laugh broke from her lips.

Todd waited for a moment, as if he needed to carefully choose each word. "As for the other. . .no, it isn't that obvious, Amy. You keep so busy with the boys that they act as a very effective smoke screen. Still, you deserved far better, and I'm sad you didn't have a safe and happy home with Joseph. I told you at the pool that day; you're a small woman and need to be protected from the rough stuff. At the time, I didn't really know how true those words were."

"I don't need anyone to protect me."

"Yes, Amy. We all do. We all need to be loved, cherished, spoiled, sheltered. From the cradle to the grave, that need never varies. You've built a wall up because those needs were not met, and you hurt too much to try again."

"You sound just like the director of the women's group."

"What group, Amy? The same one that helped you with Mike and John when they were babies?"

Her head nodded against his chest. "The shelter organized group meetings to try and help us all deal with what was happening."

"So you lived in a shelter? What made you decide to go?"

"The obstetrician—he saw. . .I. . ." She struggled to evade saying too much. Finally she blurted out, "He told me the boys would grow up to be just like Joseph if I stayed."

"He was right, Amy. You were incredibly strong to do it."

She snuggled closer and sighed.

He threaded his fingers through her curls, and his gentle touch was as soothing as his praise. The cadence of his breaths regulated hers and calmed her troubled spirit. After a few sweet moments of peace, he said, "I don't want to pry anything out of you that you're not ready to tell me. I won't take advantage of your vulnerability. When you're ready to talk, I'm here."

"It was an awful time," she whispered tightly. "I try not to remember any of it."

His hold altered very slightly and brought her deeper into the haven of his warmth. He said nothing at all.

Amy couldn't explain why, but she felt safe enough to give him a tiny glimpse behind her carefully constructed walls. "We stayed at the shelter for three months. I was six months pregnant and stayed for two months before the boys were born. They helped me to avoid Joseph. At first, we tried to get him into counseling; but he refused, and he even started carrying a gun."

His breathing hitched and his body curled ever so slightly, as if to protect her, even now—though it had happened years ago. Amy rested her cheek against him and confessed, "I'd prayed for reconciliation and healing in the marriage, but by then I couldn't put my sons at risk anymore. Joseph was killed in a trucking accident, so the women at the shelter helped me through the funeral. The boys were a full four weeks early, and I went back for a month after the delivery so they could help me."

"Sweet Amy, I'm glad they were there for you. I wish I

had been able to see you through that time. Have you gotten any help dealing with your feelings since then?"

"No. Not enough time. Not enough money. There isn't anyone who does any counseling at all for a twenty-mile radius." She shrugged. Her stomach growled.

The atmosphere in the room was too tense. Todd took advantage of the sound and chuckled. "The most pressing need seems to be to feed you. I don't want you to starve to death."

"I—" Amy paused. "Okay."

Todd stood up, still cradling her. "What were you going to say?" he asked softly.

Amy bit her lip and shook her head.

"Want me to give you a minute alone in the washroom?"

"Please!"

Chuckling, Todd asserted, "You only had to say so."

A few minutes later, as he carried her down the hall, he asked, "We can seat you at the kitchen table and put your foot up on the opposite chair, or you can lounge on the couch to eat. What do you say?"

"The couch, please."

"Your wish is my command," he proclaimed in his most gallant voice, gifting her with a toothy smile.

"Oh, dear, and to think I wasted a wish on where I'd sit," she twittered.

"So if you could have any wish at all, what would it be?" Todd lowered her onto the sofa's cushions. "Don't answer right away. Think it over while I nuke dinner. Mom made tuna casserole. Will that be okay?"

"I'm so hungry that you might even talk me into trying liver!"

"You're asking the wrong man for that." Todd made a terrible face and shuddered comically.

"You mean you aren't into torture?" As soon as the glib

words were out, Amy clapped a hand over her mouth.

Kneeling down beside the couch, Todd cupped her cheeks between his hands. His eyes regarded her steadily, and he wouldn't allow her to look away. "No, Amy. I'm into gentle pleasure. Hugging, caressing, kissing—that's my style. The only reasons I'm not courting you that way right now are simple: It would be against every ethical rule I believe in, and you're too vulnerable and drugged up right now to make any decisions. Believe me, in four weeks—after the study is over—I plan on camping at your doorstep. By then, you won't be drugged. Will you let me in, Amy?"

She found it hard to think. To breathe. Her heart thudded painfully and Amy felt so confused. Did she want him in her life? In the boys' lives?

"Are you scared of all men, or is it just me?"

"I don't know," she admitted thickly.

His fingers fanned out, and he traced her lips with one thumb while the rest of the fingers on his right hand and his palm cupped her cheek. The left hand drew her hair off to the side, his fingers combing her wayward curls and then sliding down her neck to rest lightly on her shoulder. "We have time, sweet lady. Until you feel ready, I'll keep my distance. For now, I guess we'll pass up dessert and concentrate on the main course. Tuna noodle casserole it is." Todd looked like he regretted removing his hands, but did so anyway. His control baffled her. He stood and walked toward the kitchen.

"That was wonderful," Amy sighed, putting down her fork.

"Mom can make a casserole with her eyes closed."

"Well, you reheat it with expert flair."

"Nuking things is my bachelor specialty. I end up eating a lot of fast food. I haven't been with any other family who eats home-cooked meals that are as well balanced and delicious as yours."

"Get serious, Todd."

"Think for a minute. You know Maise better than about anyone else. How often do the Tanks go out to eat, and how often does Maise cook a meal?"

Amy repositioned herself on the sofa and thought for a minute. "I never thought much about it. Maise works thirty hours a week, though."

"Sure, but you sew and monogram for a solid twenty, minimum. She has one kid. You have four!"

"So eating out is less expensive for her," Amy stated.

"You sure can try my patience, woman," Todd growled, wagging his forefinger at her.

"I don't dare do that! Otherwise I'll be reduced to crawling again!"

"I still can't believe you were actually crawling!" Todd shook his head.

"What is the old saying, 'Seeing is believing?' or perhaps 'First you have to crawl before you can walk' is more apt in this situation." She wriggled again.

"Did Mom put jumping beans in the dinner?" Todd asked, watching Amy shimmy on the couch.

"Very funny," Amy groused.

"Having trouble getting comfortable? Want to take your medicine and go back to bed?"

"Yes, I'm having trouble; and no, I refuse to be zoned out again and laze in the bed any more than I absolutely must." She moved a pillow and punched it viciously. "Why don't you tell me how the scan percentages turned out today?"

Todd sauntered over to the couch and slowly burrowed his hands between Amy and the cushions. "Yesterday you were happiest lying on your side. Let's put you that way again."

"Really—I—" Amy's protest was cut short by her gasp.

Todd simply lifted and slid her over until she was centered on the overstuffed cushions and then rolled her onto her side with ease.

"Better?" He eyed her carefully. "This way you don't have to lie on those bruises and scrapes all down your spine."

"I—um—This is fine. Really, Todd, I feel pretty decent. I don't want to be treated like—"

"Like someone special? Like someone who got hurt and needs a little bit of help here and there?"

"Once I get the cast on tomorrow, I'll show you— I'll be able to walk and take care of everything."

"Mrs. Amy Louise Independence Wilkins. Lady, you really wall yourself off. You look like the world's welterweight champ took you on—and fought dirty, to boot. You have a concussion, broken bones, and a Technicolor back. Yet, you still want to prove yourself!"

"What is wrong with being independent?"

"In small measures, it's wonderful. In huge doses, it's unhealthy. Think about the body of Christ and how we're made to complement and help one another. Serving each other is biblical, Amy. That means sometimes you have to take instead of give."

She rubbed her brow in vexation. "I know that, but—"

"Amy, you moved out because you didn't want your sons to grow into victimizers like their father. Now you're teaching them that accepting help or being interdependent is wrong. What kind of marriages will they have if that is the message you send them? It may not be as violent, but it can be incredibly crippling, too."

Thankfully, she was already lying down. Amy felt overwhelmingly dizzy and sick. Todd's words cut to the quick. She swallowed hard and buried a cheek into the cushion.

Todd took a pillow and gently tucked it under her splint to

keep it elevated. "You sometimes show them a glimpse of it Amy—trading favors with Maise or the Jacksons. That's a good start—positive. Do more of it. Allowing the ladies of the church to cook a few meals this week and having the boys see that community and friends can band together when things go wrong is a powerful message. It didn't upset them to see me carry you in the house today. They were just glad to have you home again. You're the only one who is shocked by any of the ordinary goings on."

"I don't consider having an overgrown man spending the night an ordinary occurance."

"Overgrown? Does my size scare you?"

"Want to recite the story about David and Goliath to make me feel safer?" Amy quipped weakly.

"I'll even give you a slingshot, if it would make the difference. I suppose that to someone of your slight stature, I look a bit oversized," he admitted, smoothing a finger over his mustache thoughtfully.

"A bit oversized? That first day when you showed up in your coat and tie and stepped into the entryway, I felt like a Lilliputian when Gulliver arrived!"

He slowly took her hand and cradled it in his. Their difference seemed even more apparent when contrasting the size of their hands. Todd deliberately slid his other hand on top of hers. "Amy, God designed a woman to be smaller than a man so that he could guard and shelter her. Instead of thinking of my size as a threat, I want you to think of it as a refuge. You don't ever have to be afraid of me."

"I don't want to talk about this." She snatched her hand away.

He let her go. He'd said what needed to be said, but Todd was wise enough not to delve more deeply into her pain. The way she'd cowered when startled and the fact that Amy didn't tell him what Joseph had done or what the doctor had seen to tip him off were of great significance. Her omissions served to underscore how bad things must have been. Todd forced his voice to sound casual, "Then let's talk about something else. Guess what? My accuracy rating for IDing the boys shot up to sixty-nine percent today. Explain that one."

She perked up a little. "Sixty-nine? Wow! I'm impressed. What was different?"

"I was hoping you'd help me decide that."

"Well, you've gotten used to them. . .but I would have expected a slow rise rather than a huge jump if that were the case."

"My thoughts precisely. I don't think there's any one thing that I look for on each boy. Sure, I know a few tricks. The little quirks and some of the minor oddities make it more likely to be one over the other, but still—sixty-nine!"

"Actually, seventy. You were right about Danny from the staircase earlier. How did you do that?"

"He's the lightest sleeper according to your night diary. He gets up more than the other three combined. A simple trick—playing the odds."

"So do you think it is more a matter that I'm so used to all of the quirks, I mentally calculate the odds and come out right more often? Is that it?"

"No doubt that figures in. Nonetheless, you identify them accurately when they are standing still, wearing the same clothes, and are silent. There has to be far more working here."

"The only thing that was really different today was that I was out of the picture. You had to do it yourself. I have to admit, I've often wondered if it is as much a mindset of they-are-too-similar-why-bother, so teachers and friends don't try. You didn't have me to fall back on. You were forced to sink or swim. Did the kids do any switching today, or were they straight with you?"

"They swapped like crazy once they were sure you weren't going to dry up and blow away. I think it was probably a backlash from being so concerned yesterday."

"I'm sorry they gave you a hard time, Todd."

"Don't be. I'm glad they feel comfortable enough to be themselves around me. It's the biggest compliment they could have given me. I walked in knowing full well that twins do this frequently. Now we're starting to get a notion of exactly how often, why, and what triggers such behavior. I find it challenging and it actually tickles me."

"Most often, it irritates the daylights out of me," Amy groused. "I spend all of my time trying to treat them as individuals and encouraging teachers, neighbors, and friends to treat them individually; and in one fell swoop, the little monsters mess it all up!"

"They rain on your parade, huh?"

"I guess you could say that. The thing is: I think I've been campaigning on their behalf and they don't seem to care!"

"You have the same look of frustration and irritation that my mom always wore when I walked across the newly cleaned floor with muddy shoes."

"I'll bet. More than likely, you brought in half of the yard on those monstrous feet!"

After looking down at his feet, Todd shot her a boyish grin. "Do you think they're all that big?"

"I've occasionally wondered if you have another Corvette to put on the other foot," Amy teased.

"You little pip-squeak!" He gave her a mock scowl, then noted that her face had fallen. His heart flipped over. Had he frightened her? Todd softened his voice, "What's wrong, Amy?"

"I hurt my right foot!"

"You mean just now? Did you bump it? I'll—"

"No! I mean it is my *right* foot that got hurt."

"So?" His reaction was completely blasé.

"I won't be able to drive!"

Todd let the notion sink in for a second, then shrugged. "No, you won't. So I'll drive. We got over that hurdle easily enough."

"Don't be so smug! How long will I have the cast? And you aren't always here, anyway."

"We'll find out about the length of time for the cast tomorrow. Since Mom is back, I don't need to house sit, so I'll just stay put here."

"You can't!" Her face and tone were scandalized.

"Why not?"

"You can't! I—no. Not a chance."

"Want to tell me why you're digging in your heels, or am I supposed to be a mind reader?"

"I don't want the boys growing any more attached to you than they already are."

"There won't be any difference in my exposure to them. I'm here when they get up and leave after they are asleep. Try again."

"The house isn't big enough."

"Amy, you're sleeping down here in the sewing room. There's no way you can go upstairs. I'll sleep up there so I'm available if the boys have nightmares or get sick. It's the only practical way of handling this situation."

"It isn't right! I don't want this!"

"Are you afraid other people will talk, or that we're setting a bad example for the boys, or do you fear things might heat up between us?" he asked keenly.

"Yes."

"I gave you three choices, Amy. Are you getting tired, or do you have a headache?"

"Don't patronize me. Yes, I'm tired and yes, my head is doing nasty things; but yes, I worry about all three possibilities. I don't want to get a reputation, set a dangerous precedent with the boys, or have you get any more familiar than you already have."

"Great speech. We can handle most of this. We'll put you to bed after you take something for your headache. The boys will be made to understand that our sleeping arrangements are separate. I'll behave in my most ethically pure manner, and the neighbors can go hang."

"Easy for you to say!" she cried hotly. "You'll cruise back to the university research division and leave me here to deal with all of their tales and gossip!"

"With my mom, Maise, and Pastor Jordan in your corner, are you kidding?"

Amy groaned. "Maise decided that we should get married after talking to you on the phone when she gave you my name. Driving by and seeing your Corvette cinched the relationship, as far as she was concerned. Your mother has my kids calling her 'Grandma.' Who's kidding whom? With friends like that, who needs the community gossip?"

"We could just go ahead and get married and kill the gossip dead away," Todd shot back.

"I said I had a headache. I didn't say I needed a brain transplant."

ten

"Grandma Ruth" appeared the next day and sent Amy off with Todd to see the doctor. "Stay out for lunch or something," she called to them. "I'm going to take the boys swimming and to a movie."

"Great." Amy slumped down in the seat of the car and shot Todd a dirty look.

"Don't blame me. I didn't put her up to that. My mom has excellent taste. She adores you and took to the boys in an instant. She wants to play matchmaker so we can all live happily ever after." Todd raised his palms in a "why-fight-it" gesture, then started the van. As he backed out of the driveway, he started to whistle a lilting tune. They were halfway down the street before Amy could place it. It was a song from the musical *Fiddler on the Roof,* "Matchmaker!"

Deciding to put an end to the nonsense, Amy leaned forward and turned on the radio. The oldies station was playing "The Wedding Song." She switched the dial immediately. The rock station was featuring a screeching guitar piece where an agonized voice was screaming all about love. Shuddering, she kept turning the dial and hit and stumbled onto an ad for Eileen's Bridal and Formal Wear. The classical station announcer then proclaimed that they were going to play music on the theme of unrequited love that afternoon. . . . Amy switched off the radio and slowly burned as Todd unsuccessfully choked back laughter in the other seat.

"So what do you feel like having?" Todd asked an hour and a half later.

"A big brown bag to put over my head!" Amy declared miserably.

"That would make you my lunch—" Todd oozed maddeningly.

"Listen. I'm not much in a mood for this nonsense," Amy snapped.

"Are you in a mood for Chinese? We could go to Loy's. You like the almond chicken there."

They were at a stoplight. Amy glowered out the windshield. She was in a royal snit because the doctor insisted upon applying a simple cast and wouldn't hear of putting on a walking pad or giving her a walking shoe with it. "That ankle fracture is nasty and the metatarsals shouldn't have any weight bearing at all for at least two weeks," he'd explained.

"Great. I get to be a kangaroo and hop everywhere."

"Crutches sound a bit safer, Mrs. Wilkins. Use them and schedule a visit for two weeks. We'll x-ray you then and decide where to go to from there."

"You mean I might have to use them for longer?" she asked in a horrified tone.

"We'll see."

Amy glared at the doctor, then the look swept across the room to encompass Todd. "That's exactly what I say when I know an honest answer will upset the boys."

A cackle blurted out of the doctor's mouth, and he grinned at her guiltily.

"When do I get to walk and when will the cast be off entirely?"

"At least two weeks with this cast, then probably two weeks more in another one. I'm not sure when I'll let you walk—depends on how quickly the bones knit." Amy was replaying those words as they waited for the light to change.

"Amy," Todd said softly, "wearing a cast isn't the end of the world."

"Easy for you to say."

"I've had my share of them." He smiled at her. "Now is it Loy's for Chinese or The Wharf for seafood?"

"I don't care. What do you feel like?"

Todd gave her a lopsided grin and said in an amused tone, "You might get mad if I am honest, but here goes: I'm in the mood for some crab."

Amy threw back her head and giggled uncontrollably. "Well, here I am! I'm sorry, Todd. I'm in rare form today, aren't I?"

"Just about as bad as I was when I had a cast on my right arm and missed out on the baseball playoff."

"Oh, no! How old were you?"

"Eight. I've never forgotten how frustrated I felt, though."

During the next two weeks, Amy kept reminding herself of Todd's childhood plight. It didn't help much, but there was little other solace to be found for the fact that she couldn't take a shower. Ruth was rather clever at problem solving. She came over and had Todd lift Amy onto the kitchen counter. With her stretched out full length, Ruth washed Amy's hair in the sink. It felt wonderful. Thereafter, Todd willingly washed her hair, himself.

Todd did a lot. Too much, if Amy were asked. He drove them everywhere—to soccer practice, to the grocery store, to church. Amy was settled into the sewing room for the time being, and Todd used her bedroom as his own. Maise had come over and removed Amy's lingerie and some of her clothes so Todd would have someplace to put his clothes. Maise whispered to Amy, "You couldn't be doing a better job of snaring him, gal. What a hunk!"

"Maise. . ." Amy gave her a nasty look.

"Okay. Okay. Just let the idea grow on you awhile," she threw in for good measure.

Amy's shoulders and arms were tired and sore from the crutches. Every evening, Todd would rub them, but she was loath to allow him the opportunity. "The bruises and scabs on your back are too sore," he said the first time she refused him, "no crutches for a few days."

"But—"

"I can carry you wherever you need to go." He folded his arms across his chest and ended the conversation. After enduring that treatment and hopping whenever she could to avoid the contact, Amy finally agreed that she would submit to a nightly rub if she were given the crutches. Having him lift and carry her did strange things to her, and the feelings didn't bear too close of a scrutiny.

Todd insisted that Amy stop wearing the laser set. "We already have piles of very consistent data on your accuracy and patterns. I don't think it will make a difference. At this point, the question is—can you help me improve my stats? I need to be the one wearing the laser."

Todd had good and bad days in identifying the boys. He had a terrible time differentiating them on the soccer field. At the kitchen table, he was right almost all of the time. If the boys were fairly close by, slight differences in personality trends he'd seen in the tests cued him as to the fact that it was Ken because of his emotional makeup or John because of his sense of humor. Overall, he was in the high sixties and occasionally in the mid-seventies with his name assignments, an appreciable jump and significant to the research. "I believe our data indicates that identification is a transferable skill," he told Amy.

She gave him a warm smile. "A victory?"

"Definitely. . .at least for us," he added. "I'm putting

together a list of things that might be cues for other sets of twins. We listed some of them in my original hypothesis, but other determining factors are real surprises. I have a few associates at other research facilities that are ready to implement the concepts to see if they can be applied to other pairs."

Todd kept a list of the cues that made determining identity easier. "We'll give the lists to the boys' teachers and see if they make a difference," he said to Amy late one evening. They were looking at the computer printouts and comparing the trends. Amy yawned. "Okay. Enough for you. To bed." Todd stood up and snatched her out of her chair.

"I can walk, you know," she said dryly.

"Yeah with those crutches."

"We see Doc in two days. I'm hoping."

"But until then, you're hopping," Todd teased lightheartedly. "I'll be kind of sad if he allows you to walk. I like having an excuse to hold you." He set her down by the sink so she could brush her teeth. Looking at her reflection in the mirror, Todd leaned down and said, "Don't blush, sweet Amy. I'll devise reasons to carry you regardless." He left at the sound of her muted gasp.

After Todd had gone to bed, Amy couldn't sleep. She hopped back into the living room and looked at the information on the computer screen. Todd had put everything into simple-to-read flow sheets and graphs, so following the trends and progress would be easy enough. It intrigued her to no end. Her leg was throbbing, though. Deciding that she ought to put it up, she hit the print button and had all of the information transfer onto paper so she could lie in bed and read. The printer was fairly quiet, and she muffled the noise further by closing the doors. After printing out the last sheet, she set aside the disk, turned off the power to the computer, and went to her bed. Suddenly far more tired than she thought, she slid the huge pile of papers into a drawer and fell asleep.

Todd got up earlier than she did the next morning. He had the computer on and was deep into his work when Amy called everyone to the breakfast table. By putting the waffle iron on the table, she could sit and make breakfast. Todd and she tarried over breakfast for a few minutes. A big commotion in the living room brought them to their feet.

"I'm going to tell!"

"It's your fault!"

"Hey! What gives here?" Todd asked.

Amy let out a yelp and blanched. "Amy?" Todd turned to her.

"Oh, Todd! Your computer!" she cried.

"Mike pushed me!" Ken blamed.

"You weren't supposed to have juice in the living room, stupid!"

"Quiet!" Todd boomed.

"Go sit over by the fireplace and don't say another word," Amy hissed. Dan and Ken were both trying to sop up orange juice from the keyboard. The computer screen made funny patterns and a crackling noise.

"Guys, don't touch it. I need to cut the power off. I don't want you to get electrocuted," Todd commanded in a tight voice. He pulled the plugs swiftly and they began to try to clean up the mess and salvage what they could.

"I'm so sorry, Todd," Amy sobbed.

"Give it up, Amy. A machine isn't worth that kind of grief. It was an accident, albeit an expensive one." Todd ran his hand through his hair. All of that work! All of his data! "Boy am I glad I kept a backup disk!"

"What's a backup thing?" John asked, his voice all choked up.

"It is what is going to save my neck, little man. It is a thin plastic and metal thing that holds computer information."

"You mean like this?" John picked up the topic of conversation, using a large red horseshoe magnet.

"Oh, no!" Todd's face bled to the color of beeswax. "You've erased it! That magnet! All of my work—" He took the disk and collapsed onto the couch.

"What's wrong, Todd?" Kenny asked.

"Boys!" Amy barked. "Go to your rooms."

"All of it erased," Todd said in a shocked voice. He turned a disbelieving face to Amy. "Magnets erase disks. I never thought—"

"John Robert, Michael Alan to your room! You, too, Daniel James and Kenneth Andrew. *Now! And shut your doors.*" Amy was both frightened and appalled. All of the hours and weeks of work, gone in an instant. Todd was going to be mad. Mad meant danger. She wanted the boys out of harm's way.

Hearing the tone of voice and the use of all of their middle names, the boys bolted. Amy collapsed and cowered in a chair as the bedroom doors slammed.

Todd rubbed his hands across his face and rose. "I don't believe it!" he thundered in a furious tone. His momentary shock was wearing off. "I don't believe it!" he repeated, rubbing a large hand over the nape of his neck. "Every single bit of data—every count, fact, theory, gone! All of it!" He paced the length of the room twice, his strides long and forceful. "The whole study blown to bits!" He wheeled around.

Eyes wide with terror, Amy huddled in the chair. If it weren't for her cast, she would have run with the kids. A wordless sound of panic erupted from her as Todd came closer.

It was as if a bucket of ice-cold water had been sloshed over him. Todd stared at her, horrified at the thought that she feared him. His anger evaporated, the study completely forgotten. "Amy—" he choked out, going over to her at once. She pulled away. "No, Amy," he whispered. He used his superior strength against her only in that he lifted her rigid body from her chair. Pivoting, he sat down and cradled her, encompassing her in his arms and groaning, "Oh, Amy, no. Nothing is more important than you and the boys. Nothing. I didn't mean to scare you, honey. It's okay." He crooned to her and stroked her back and smoothed her hair.

When she finally realized the beating she had feared wasn't going to materialize, Amy burst into tears. Todd held her until she was all cried out.

"No matter how bad things are, I'll never be violent," he vowed. "Don't you see, honey? Love isn't that way."

"But all of your work—"

Todd groaned and a pained expression contorted his features. He shook his head and looked deep into her eyes. "Amy, I won't pretend it isn't a huge blow, but the study wasn't half as important as you and the kids. The biggest victories this summer weren't that we learned to tell the boys apart. The biggest victories this summer were the real miracles—of me finding you and the boys, and of me rededicating my life to Christ. If I can't have everything, I'm still left with the things I value most."

She curled more closely and let his words sink in. All at once, she yelped, "Oh, my!" and struggled to get away from him. He held tight.

"No, Amy. Don't run."

"Let go!" She wriggled madly. "You don't understand!"

"Make me understand," he insisted, gently clamping a hand at the nape of her neck and turning her to face him.

"I want to go to the sewing room!"

"You aren't making any sense!"

"Antares Todd Avery, take me to the sewing room!" Whether it was her use of his name, her tone of voice, or her facial expression, he wasn't sure. At any rate, Todd stood and carried her to the designated room. "Over to my dresser."

Complying with her demands, Todd asked, "What are you up to?"

As she wrenched the drawer open and thrust her hand inside, Amy proclaimed, "This!" She produced all of the papers she'd printed off the night before and thrust them at Todd's chest. "Your work! I copied it last night so I could read it in bed!"

"*What?!*"

Todd deposited Amy onto the twin bed and she waved the papers in his face. "I copied it! Every single bit of it! I copied all of it because looking at the computer gives me a headache and my leg throbs!"

Todd let out a whoop and hugged her tightly. The papers were pressed between them in a mad jumble, and they rustled as Todd lowered his head and claimed Amy's mouth.

The sensations were overwhelming. Amy clung to him as her world tipped upside down. He plied her mouth with an exuberant kiss that then softened to seductive nibbles at the corners and then traced the contours of the bow shape of her lips. His hands threaded through her hair, cradling her head and allowing him to exert gentle pressure with his lips that made her insides turn to warm mush. Breathless, he finally pulled away.

Amy sagged against him and finally came to her senses. She inhaled a long, choppy breath.

Mindless of the papers, Todd slid his arms around her and cuddled her close. "See? Being together can bring gentle pleasure, Amy." His voice was husky and shook slightly. "Oh, honey, you feel so right in my arms. I'm so thankful God brought us together."

Amy shivered. The papers rustled. "I think we'd better take care of things—like the papers and the boys."

Todd laughed a deep, throaty laugh which rumbled deep in his chest so that Amy could feel the vibrations. "Come on. I think we'd better handle the boys together." He sat up and stared down at her. "You sure are a beautiful woman, Amy." His eyes caressed her warmly.

Feeling her cheeks go hot, Amy turned away. Todd pulled her back. "Don't run from me, lady. I'll keep following you. Two more weeks, and the study is over. After that, you're at my mercy."

He had to have felt her shudder. His arms tightened. "No, Amy. I love you. After the study is over, I'll be free to interact with you and the boys without any artificial restraints.

"I'll never hurt you, Amy. I'll never push you to give more than you have, either. Not even once have I been violent with any woman, and I can't imagine stooping to that level. As for the boys, I suppose it isn't very romantic for me to bring them up when I'm trying to capture your heart, but I understand your devotion to them. They are wonderful kids, Amy. I'll treat them like they're my own."

"I'm not sure—"

"Nothing in life is guaranteed, little lady. Two weeks." He leaned over her and kissed her so gently that she, herself, was tempted to deepen the contact. She had never experienced such feelings and the powerful emotion left her shaken. As he lifted his head, Todd repeated, "Two weeks."

The next month was a blur. They went back-to-school shopping, and even though Amy was able to walk on her new cast, Todd insisted she ride in a wheelchair through the mall. She felt terribly conspicuous; but the boys loved sitting on her lap as Todd pushed it, and they were able to hang all of the bags from the handles. At one store, each boy chose five pairs of jeans apiece. Todd got a pair for himself, as well. The salesgirl nearly came unhinged as she rang up a single sale of twenty-one pairs of pants in one fell swoop. Amy didn't realize that Todd had substituted his credit card for hers because the wheelchair kept her below the high counter level. As Todd began to sign the charge slip, she grabbed for it.

"Is something wrong, Mrs. Avery?" the sales girl asked.

The boys all broke into gales of laughter. "Mrs. Avery!" they nearly shouted.

"Hush!" she hissed at the boys.

"Hey, Mom! You're turning red!"

Amy mumbled something, and Todd wheeled them out. "I like the sound of that—Mrs. Avery," he mused softly in her ear.

"No secrets!" Michael huffed in outrage, quoting a family rule that Todd was breaking.

"You got me there, Mike. I guess I owe you a soda for that one." Todd directed the wheelchair over to the food court and situated them at two adjoining tables. "Come on, Dan and John. You help me." A few moments later, the threesome returned with enormous root beer floats. After the break, they plowed through Sears to purchase underwear and socks. The next three stops yielded shirts of all varieties, and then they went to the shoe store.

The boys returned to school with accompanying tip sheets for the teachers on identifying characteristics. Things were going slowly, but the boys reported that the teachers actually seemed to be assigning their names more accurately than in the past.

Todd spent long hours completing his study before submitting it to the research panel. They were suitably impressed. The study quickly garnered considerable attention and was hailed as a victory in separating and distinguishing factors that promoted recognition of identities of twins. The findings were released with the standard proviso that the identities of the subjects were to be kept secret. Amy felt relieved, and

Todd kissed her as he underlined that particular paragraph. "I think we need some time and privacy, and I'm not willing to share all of you with anyone else," he proclaimed in a throaty, possessive tone.

A few days later, Todd stopped in to see Amy. She didn't answer the door, yet her van was in the driveway. Concerned, he went around to the backyard and gained entry into the house through the kitchen door. He found Amy dozing on the couch. She woke with a start.

"Whoa! It's just me," Todd said quietly. He held her shoulder, gently guiding her to lie back on the couch. Then, he looked into her startled face. "I didn't mean to scare you. I knocked, but you didn't answer." He gently combed his fingers through her short curls. "It's not like you to nap. Aren't you feeling well?"

A delicate pink suffused her cheeks. "I'm fine."

"Okay," he said softly. The almost imperceptible hesitation between those two words told him plenty. "I'll brew you some tea to help your tummy."

Later, he kept an arm around her as she curled up by his side and sipped the tea. "Amy, you know I love you. I love the boys, too. I want us to be a family, and I truly feel God brought us together. Marry me."

She set the mug on the coffee table with a thump and buried her face in her hands.

"Amy?"

She shook her head. "I can't. I just can't! I don't—" her voice trailed off helplessly.

"—Know if you can bear the thought of being intimate?" Todd finished for her with a gentle tone. She nodded. He enfolded her in his arms and felt her shudder. "I think we'd better talk."

Amy went completely rigid.

Rather than fighting her or prolonging the situation, Todd simply picked her up and slid her across his lap. He held her gently. "I'm not letting go of you," he assured her. He raised his hand to stroke her cheek and she flinched. "Amy?"

She wouldn't meet his eyes. "Go," she said thickly, averting her face.

The couch creaked as he leaned back and gathered her more closely. He cupped her head to his shoulder and gently brushed his fingers across her temple. Her breathing was harsh in the silence of the room. "I hope you know I'll always be tender with you," he said quietly. "You've reclaimed all of the other areas of your life, Amy. Why don't we ask God for healing? He can make you whole even in this. Have you ever prayed about it?"

She shook her head. "There was no reason."

"There's every reason now." He folded his hand over hers. "Dear Father in Heaven, You know the heavy burden Amy has carried all of these years. You know the scars she bears. You are the Mighty Healer, and I ask You to touch her and relieve her pain. Give her peace and calm her fears. Do Your work in her heart so she can live a full and complete life. Just as You've cleansed us from all unrighteousness, cleanse Amy of the memories that prevent her from experiencing the rich life she deserves. We give You honor and praise for this, and for all of the victories in our lives, Amen."

She wept softly as he prayed. Afterward, Todd wiped away her tears. "I'm going to kiss you, sweet lady." He teased her lips gently, plying them with tenderness that was so fragile that she could hardly breathe. His lips brushed over her salty tear tracks and teased her temples.

When he lifted his face from her burning skin, Amy let out a small sigh. "I don't know what to do."

"You love me, don't you?"

She looked at him and felt a glow she'd never thought possible. Slowly, Amy nodded. "Yes, I do—but I don't know if that'll be enough."

"Step out in faith." He smiled. "Come with me to a jewelry store so that we can buy your ring. I'd like to trade the temporary sparkle of those laser rings for the permanent dazzle of a diamond."

As they were out shopping for a ring, Amy suddenly stopped and asked, "Todd, you've said you like having the boys. How do you feel about more children?"

He smiled. "I read Psalm 127 this morning. It said children are a blessing from God. Something about sons being like arrows. Verse five said, 'Happy is the man whose quiver is full,' and that suited me just fine."

"I want you to be happy," she said, "but aren't you afraid I might have twins again?"

"The odds of that are less likely than you winning the lottery. Still, there are a few women who are what we term 'super fecund.' No one knows why, but they have multiples time after time."

She laughed. "Since I've never even bought a lottery ticket, I won't worry."

⋅❧

Two weeks later, they were married. All four boys escorted Amy down the aisle and stood at the altar. She trembled slightly as Todd placed the wedding band next to the oval diamond engagement ring. Her pale blue tea-length dress whispered as they knelt for prayer, and Pastor Jordan beamed brightly as he pronounced them man and wife. The kiss was modest for a couple of reasons—to preserve Amy's sense of propriety, and to avoid the disgusting noises young boys make when witnessing signs of affection.

Later that night in the honeymoon suite, Amy steeled herself before opening the bathroom door. For all of Todd's promises to be gentle, she was still afraid. "Lord, please, I ask you for courage to overcome," she prayed.

As soon as she walked out, Todd held out his hands to her and softly praised, "You're beautiful, little wife."

She reached out and took both of his hands. His touch was warm and reassuring.

"Amy, we belong to one another now. Sharing ourselves is a gift. Your touch pleases me so much. I hope my touch feels as good to you." He drew her close and ran his hands along her back. He cupped one side of her face and lowered his lips to hers. Slowly, she raised her hand and curled it around his neck.

A full hour later, Amy nestled close beside him. Todd whispered his love and gently kissed her hair. Beneath her palm, his heart beat a steady cadence of love for her and for the Lord who had granted her victory over her fears.

epilogue

Six months later, Todd's secretary handed him a cryptic message. He had set up a private practice in the community and still did research for the university on the side, when time permitted. Amy had been right—no Christian psychological counseling was available for a solid twenty-mile radius.

His practice was thriving. Dr. Garvey had referred several families to him. Today's message from the physician stated that he had a client in need of a hospital visit. Could Todd stop by Room 230 at five fifteen?

Todd dialed Amy. "Do you mind if I'm late tonight, honey? Doc Garvey has someone in the hospital, and the family can meet at five fifteen."

"Okay. Do you think you could pick up some milk on the way home? I don't think we have enough for breakfast."

"Sure. You sound funny. Are you okay?"

"I'm frazzled and tired. I have to ice five dozen cupcakes for the Valentine's Day parties at school. I'd rather just snuggle up on the couch with you."

"Hold that thought!" He laughed.

At five fifteen, Todd walked into the maternity unit of the hospital. "Todd!" Dr. Garvey met him and shook hands. He drew him off to the side. "This woman is having a sonogram. They detected two heartbeats in the obstetrician's office, and she isn't sure how her husband is going to handle the news."

Todd's face split into a smile. "I guess this is right up my alley, eh?

"Definitely. Room 230."

"What are their names?"

Just then a nurse came up and diverted Dr. Garvey. "Excuse me—" he apologized. A second later, he shrugged and mouthed, "Room 230."

Todd walked down the hall and tapped lightly on the door. "Come on in," a voice called out.

Todd opened the door and introduced himself to the party behind the drawn curtain.

"Please come on around," the technician invited. "I think you can wedge yourself in over by the window."

Todd sidestepped an electrical cord and moved beyond the curtain. Raising his gaze from the floor to the bed, he stopped dead in his tracks. *"Amy?"*

"Surprise!" She giggled.

"You were out of town last month," she explained when he gave her a look of disbelief. "I wasn't sure, so I just let you assume that we weren't pregnant. Dr. Avington is about ready to die." She pointed to the ultrasound screen.

"Twins!" he said far more loudly than he had planned. He flushed and kissed her soundly.

"You promised me that I stood a better chance of winning the lottery than having twins again," Amy scolded, but her face was creased with an excited smile.

Staring at the screen, he asked, "What are they?"

"It's too soon to tell."

"I can tell you now from the scan that they are identical—they share the placenta," informed the technician.

Amy and Todd exchanged glances and broke out laughing. Todd gave her another kiss and quoted, "Happy is the man whose quiver is full."

A Letter To Our Readers

Dear Reader:

In order that we might better contribute to your reading enjoyment, we would appreciate your taking a few minutes to respond to the following questions. We welcome your comments and read each form and letter we receive. When completed, please return to the following:

Rebecca Germany, Fiction Editor
Heartsong Presents
PO Box 719
Uhrichsville, Ohio 44683

1. Did you enjoy reading *Twin Victories?*
   ❏ Very much. I would like to see more books
     by this author!
   ❏ Moderately
     I would have enjoyed it more if _____
     _____
     _____

2. Are you a member of **Heartsong Presents**? Yes ❏ No ❏
   If no, where did you purchase this book?_____
   _____

3. How would you rate, on a scale from 1 (poor) to 5 (superior), the cover design?_____

4. On a scale from 1 (poor) to 10 (superior), please rate the following elements.

   _____ Heroine   _____ Plot

   _____ Hero   _____ Inspirational theme

   _____ Setting   _____ Secondary characters

5. These characters were special because_____

_____

_____

6. How has this book inspired your life?_____

_____

_____

7. What settings would you like to see covered in future **Heartsong Presents** books?_____

_____

_____°

8. What are some inspirational themes you would like to see treated in future books?_____

_____

_____

9. Would you be interested in reading other **Heartsong Presents** titles?   Yes ❏   No ❏

10. Please check your age range:
    ❏ Under 18   ❏ 18-24   ❏ 25-34
    ❏ 35-45   ❏ 46-55   ❏ Over 55

11. How many hours per week do you read?_____

Name _____

Occupation _____

Address _____

City _____ State _____ Zip _____

ESCAPE

to the land of ancient history with pristine blue waters and white architecture. Athens resident Melanie Panagiotopoulos allows the reader to explore biblical history along with modern lifestyle and romance in a contemporary collection of three complete novels and one novella of inspirational romance. In *Odyssey of Love,* Kristen and Paul search for the meaning of life and love among the ruins of the Acropolis. Niki and Phil look for the road to peace and forgiveness at the origin of the Olympic Games and along the biblical shores of Cenchrea in *Race of Love.* For Melissa and Luke, in *Fortress of Love,* something important is missing from their relationship that they will explore in the shadow of the ancient Chlemoutsi Castle. Finally, Christina and Dino search for the truth about the *Christmas Baby* amidst the ancient streets of Athens.

paperback, 464 pages, 5 ¾₆" x 8"

·······Presents·······

Great Inspirational Romance at a Great Price!

Heartsong Presents books are inspirational romances in contemporary and historical settings, designed to give you an enjoyable, spirit-lifting reading experience. You can choose wonderfully written titles from some of today's best authors like Veda Boyd Jones, Yvonne Lehman, Tracie Peterson, Debra White Smith, and many others.

When ordering quantities less than twelve, above titles are $2.95 each.
Not all titles may be available at time of order.

Hearts♥ng Presents
Love Stories Are Rated G!

That's for godly, gratifying, and of course, great! If you love a thrilling love story, but don't appreciate the sordidness of some popular paperback romances, **Heartsong Presents** is for you. In fact, **Heartsong Presents** is the *only inspirational romance book club* featuring love stories where Christian faith is the primary ingredient in a marriage relationship.

Sign up today to receive your first set of four, never before published Christian romances. Send no money now; you will receive a bill with the first shipment. You may cancel at any time without obligation, and if you aren't completely satisfied with any selection, you may return the books for an immediate refund!

Imagine. . .four new romances every four weeks—two historical, two contemporary—with men and women like you who long to meet the one God has chosen as the love of their lives. . .all for the low price of $9.97 postpaid.

To join, simply complete the coupon below and mail to the address provided. **Heartsong Presents** romances are rated G for another reason: They'll arrive *Godspeed!*

I dedicate this book to the man who dares to share my dreams, laughs with me, holds me when I cry, and makes ordinary days worthwhile—My love, my husband, Christopher Roland Hake.

A note from the author:
I love to hear from my readers! You may correspond with me by writing: **Cathy Marie Hake**
Author Relations
PO Box 719
Uhrichsville, OH 44683

ISBN 1-57748-756-7

TWIN VICTORIES

Cover illustration by Kevin McClain.

PRINTED IN THE U.S.A.

Twin
Victories

Cathy Marie Hake

Heartsong Presents

CATHY MARIE HAKE is a Southern California native who loves her work as a nurse and Lamaze teacher. She and her husband have a daughter, a son, and a dog, so life is never dull or quiet. Cathy Marie considers herself a sentimental packrat, collecting antiques and Hummel figurines. She otherwise keeps busy with reading, writing, baking, and being a prayer warrior. "I am easily distracted during prayer, so I devote certain tasks and chores to specific requests or persons so I can keep faithful in my prayer life."

A surprise visit.

The doorbell rang. Amy opened one eye to look at the clock before she rolled over and pulled the pillow over her head. Six A.M. on Saturday morning. The clock read six A.M. Who would be so insane as to come to her door at such an early hour? She let out a muffled groan, yawned, and burrowed her cheek into the flower sprigged percale bed sheet.

"Mom, some guy is on the porch," Mike announced from her door.

"Tell him to go away," she mumbled.

"Wow!" Johnny's voice bellowed at top volume from downstairs.

Seconds later, a much deeper voice sounded from her doorway, "I bribed my way inside with doughnuts. I'm here to band the kids—"

Amy shrieked and bolted upright, clutching the blankets up to her neck. She and the intrusive visitor stared at each other. "Dr. Avery! What are you doing here?"